About the author

Nik Devlin lives in Crystal Palace and doesn't go to the gym as often as he should.

Photograph: AKTII/Erica Choi.

Very Very Old:

Stories of the Immortals

Nik Devlin

Very Very Old:

Stories of the Immortals

Vanguard Press

A CIP catalogue record for this title is
available from the British Library.

ISBN 978 1 78465 841 0

Vanguard Press is an imprint of
Pegasus Elliot MacKenzie Publishers Ltd.
www.pegasuspublishers.com

First Published in 2020

Vanguard Press
Sheraton House Castle Park
Cambridge England

Printed & Bound in Great Britain

Dedication

To Edwina, my love, my life.

Acknowledgements

Big thanks to my parents, Peter and Zoe, my sister, Petra, and my wife, Edwina, for reading the stories and giving me huge encouragement.

Charles Bridger in London

It only took Jess a moment to figure out why the man's face seemed so familiar. He looked an awful lot like the man in that old photo, the silver framed one showing three people standing on the front steps of a mid-Victorian style townhouse. The picture stood near the back of a forest of photos on top of her baby grand piano, the oldest pictures at the back, the newest at the front, from early twentieth century monochrome photos of ancestors standing stiffly and mostly unsmiling, to full colour digital prints of contemporaries and descendants smiling, laughing, and in some cases in mid-air snowboard action shots. The inscription on the back of that particular photo said, *Mr Benjamin and Mrs Dulcie Fullerton and Mr David Bridger, 57 Church Road, Crystal Palace, London, February 1930* in blue fountain pen. Family lore had it that Bridger was a lodger with Old Ben and Dulcie; he'd lived in the annexe for about a year, then moved on. She'd asked Grandma Sally about Bridger when she was still alive, but Sally had never met him; he'd been and gone before she was born in 1932. Sally hadn't known who'd taken the photo, or who had written the inscription on the back.

Jess had never met her great grandmother. Dulcie had died a couple of years before she was born. Most of her family agreed that she looked very, very like her; and having seen a couple of photos of Dulcie as a young woman, she had to agree. She did however have one or two memories of Old Ben, her great grandfather. She remembered a ghostly, white-bearded, stooped, old wisp of a man who lived in the annexe behind number 57. She remembered his thin, hoarse, high-pitched wheeze of a voice, and the smell of pipe tobacco and aniseed. He'd died in 1986, when she was just five.

And now, in the little cafe across the road from number 57, where she lived with her husband John and the kids, Anthony, Ben and Rachel, she was looking at a man who looked just like the David Bridger in the photo. Sitting at a table near hers, he was scribbling in a notebook with a mechanical pencil. The man looked up from his notes, and looked directly at her. An eyebrow rose, and a faint smile appeared. She smiled back uncertainly. "Good morning," he said. Then he took an envelope out of the brown leather briefcase that was lying on the table beside his notebook. "I wonder if I have here a photo of your great grandparents."

Her mind reeled. "Wha… what? My great… how do you…?"

"I'm sorry, that was dreadfully rude of me." He rose and came over to her table. He indicated the seat opposite her. "My name's Charles Bridger. May I?"

"Bridger? Did you say Bridger? Are you related to… Erm, yes, yes, sit down, but please, please explain?" she stammered.

"*Mr Benjamin and Mrs Dulcie Fullerton and Mr David Bridger, 57 Church Road, Crystal Palace, London, February 1930,*" he recited as he sat, placing his coffee cup carefully in front of him. His face, exactly the same as the David Bridger in the photo, even close up, was patrician, yet kindly, a lock of blonde hair falling over his smooth forehead. He seemed to be about forty years old, reminding her of a boyfriend at uni who had been to public school; he'd been nicknamed Phil the Greek for his resemblance to a young Duke of Edinburgh.

"Yes! Yes, I do have a photo with that written on the back! That's number 57 across the road. I live there."

He opened the envelope, and took out a photo that she saw immediately was the twin of the one near the back of the piano. He slid it across the table to her. She looked at the familiar image, then turned it over to see the same inscription written in the same ink by the same hand.

"This is… this is amazing. This is the same photo, the same handwriting. I take it this David Bridger is an ancestor of yours."

Mr Bridger smiled. "Yes," he said. "He was my great grandfather."

"And he lodged with my great grandparents," she said.

"Yes, for a year or so in 1929 and 1930. They became, according to his diaries, good friends. And here we are now, looking just like them."

"Yes, everyone's always said I'm the spit of Dulcie."

"And your name is…?"

"Oh, I'm so sorry, my name is Jessica, Jessica Fullerton. Everyone calls me Jess." She held out her hand, and he shook it. His hand was smooth and warm, and there was a feeling of strength held in check about it.

"Please to meet you Jess. Interesting to note that you're in the same house your great grandparents lived in."

"It's been in the family for five generations now, if you count my kids. My husband John moved in when we got married. It was originally built in the 1860s."

"And your parents are still around?"

"Yes, but they're off on one of those very long world cruises at the moment, been away for months. We Skyped the other day, they're in Sri Lanka, they're loving it."

"It is a splendid country." He lapsed into silence, and she broke it by asking the obvious question.

"So, what brings you here?"

He sipped his coffee for a moment, looking across the road. "Historical research, though maybe this bit is sort of a pilgrimage too. I've been out of the country for some years: Asia, the Far East, the Americas. I came back a fortnight ago, and am now engaged in researching a sort of family history." His laugh made a warm, comfortable sound.

"I have some of David's diaries, you see. And I was sitting here debating knocking on your front door to see who lived in number 57 these days, and I saw you come out, and I saw the resemblance to Dulcie. You know, from the photo. And you came in and sat down near me and I couldn't help but take a chance on talking to you. And very glad I am that I did too." He smiled.

"And have you found out anything interesting about David Bridger?"

"It seems he worked as a mechanic in Benjamin Fullerton's garage up the road. Motorcars were, well, not exactly in their infancy in this country, but they were still few and far between. But David Bridger had worked on them in America, it was quite a saleable trade to have in London in the 1920s."

"How did they meet?"

"According to his diaries, David and Benjamin got talking in a hotel bar shortly after he'd arrived from the US. David told him all about the cars he'd worked on in Chicago and New York, but confided that he was getting short on readies and looking for a job. Benjamin needed a mechanic, and he was a trusting soul, so he offered David a job and a billet there and then. Benjamin and Dulcie and Benjamin's parents lived in the main house, David lived in the annexe. While David was here, he became good friends with Benjamin and Dulcie, but he lost touch with them a few years after he moved on. His diaries are somewhat sporadic after he left the UK but it seems he travelled in the East, then settled down in New Zealand. As for the Fullertons, I do know that Benjamin and Dulcie subsequently had a son called Francis and a daughter called Sally."

"Yep, my Great Uncle Frank, he died in the war. Sally was my grandmother. Amazing lady, a real force of nature. She passed away in 2008."

"I'm sorry to hear that. What about Dulcie and Benjamin?"

"She died in '76, Benjamin in '86. I just about remember him."

He looked across the road again, and Jess felt there was something wistful in his face, like he was pining after something long gone. He turned back. "My ancestor says in his diaries that this area had been very fashionable at the turn of the century, what with the Crystal Palace itself having been brought up from Hyde Park, but that it was a bit in decline by the time he lived here. The Palace itself was falling to bits, and there was local talk about it being pulled down and sold for scrap. Of course it burned down in 1936, by which time much of it was off limits for safety reasons."

"Probably just as well," said Jess. "Can you imagine how tempting a target it would have been to the Luftwaffe during the Blitz? Big shiny, sparkly thing glinting in the moonlight!"

"Absolutely. He also writes, interestingly enough, that this cafe was open even then, when he lived across the road. It's been a cafe for many years it seems. But then you probably know that."

"Yes, it's a bit of a local institution. It's been part of my family's life since, well, ever; Sally used to sit me on her lap and buy me a hot chocolate here when I was a little girl. I still come in a couple of days a week, and the family almost always has breakfast here on Saturdays. I'm writing a magazine article today, and I kind of dried up, so I popped across. Great little place." She sipped her coffee. "Do you know who took the photo?"

"I don't know. A passer-by maybe?"

"What about the handwriting? None of the family knows who wrote it."

"I'm pretty sure it was David himself, it's not unlike the handwriting in his diaries. But look, I mustn't take up any more of your time, and I have a date with an archivist at the British Museum. A Bridger acquitted himself well at the Battle of Vigo Bay in 1702, and his papers describing the engagement are in the collection there." He stood, and picked up his briefcase. "It's been a happy accident meeting you, Jess."

"Oh, yes, it's been lovely to meet you too, it's not every day you meet someone who looks the spit of someone from, what? — an eighty-six-year-old photo." And that was when she had the idea.

They stood on the front steps of number 57, side by side, in the same positions David Bridger and Dulcie Fullerton had stood eighty-six years ago, watching the timer on her iPhone's screen count down a couple of metres away, propped up on the brick wall at the side of the steps. Then it made that camera noise, and there they were on the screen, Charles and Jess, looking like David and Dulcie. It occurred to her that Charles's brown suit was quite old fashioned, and her skirt and sweater could, in the right light, look a bit 1920s. She was already planning to display the two photos together.

"If you give me your mobile number or your email address, I can send the picture to you. It would look great in your written history," Jess said.

"That's very good of you Jess, but I don't yet have a mobile phone. It's one of those things I need to get organised about. Perhaps I could call back when I have one and let you know. But now, I'm afraid I must dash."

"OK, but please do pop by again. The kids would be fascinated to meet you. Maybe I could show you around."

"And I'd love to meet them." He held out his hand and they shook again. "Goodbye, Jess, it's been a fortuitous meeting." He smiled, then turned and walked down the steps. At the bottom he turned. His face was

18

very serious now, almost sad. "Ben and Dulcie Fullerton," he said, "they were good people. They were good people." Then he walked away down Church Road. Jess watched him till he was out of sight, then went back into the house.

Around the corner on Westow Street, Bridger stepped into a minicab office and ordered a car to the British Library. As the driver led him to the car and he climbed into the back seat, he pondered the meeting with Jess. He was glad he'd bypassed her offer to come in; he didn't know how he'd have taken to being in the house again after all this time. And he was glad he'd lied about the mobile phone. Having a copy of the picture Jess's phone had taken would have made it all the more bittersweet.

He shouldn't really have said that last line, it must have sounded, well, odd. It was a fact though; Ben and Dulcie were good people. They were kind enough to take him in when he was on his uppers, his paper fortune wiped out in the Wall Street Crash. Forced to leave the US hurriedly, he'd worked his passage on a second-rate passenger ship back to Europe, docking in Southampton and travelling up to London in a third class railway carriage, meeting Benjamin in a hotel bar at Waterloo station. He'd worked hard at Fullerton's garage too, becoming a trusted employee quickly; he had a gift with motorcars, and the Fullertons' well-heeled customers liked his attention to detail and his friendly manner. He enjoyed his life with the Fullertons, but in the summer of 1930, he'd gone to a very discreet private bank in Paris and, playing the part of his own son, taken out the modest deposit of gold he'd put there in 1880 and converted it into money orders, traveller's cheques, bank drafts and hard currency.

His initial plan, on arrival in the UK from America, had been to keep travelling eastwards: France, Germany, maybe Russia, definitely Japan (he hadn't, after all, been there since some time in the 1600s), but meeting Benjamin, and especially Dulcie, had put those plans on hold for a while. But a year or so later he changed his mind, and decided to start travelling again. So he made up a story about a lucky win at a casino, and another about a yearning to travel in Asia, and announced his departure to the Fullertons. A week before he left, he'd used the timer on his new camera to take that photo, setting it on a tripod on the pavement, and had given them a print. Then, after a last night sitting up with them in the living room, smoking cigarettes, playing jazz on the piano and gramophone and drinking beer and whisky, he'd left London once again, and gone off in search of adventure.

Benjamin had been saddened when he told them he was leaving; Dulcie had been devastated, but Charles, or David, as they knew him, had been determined to go, as he knew he was falling more and more in love with Dulcie and he suspected she had feelings for him. Beyond a handshake at the start of their relationship and a brief hug at the very end, there had never been any physical contact, but the signs were there.

Immortality was all very well, he told himself with a sigh, but there was only so much heartache a man could stand, and only so many lies one could tell. He didn't know precisely what age he was, though since some of his earliest memories were of falling hopelessly in love with a young slave woman in the court of the Emperor Claudius, he knew he was at least two thousand years old.

There were many more like him too; in the 1950s, for instance, he'd lived for a few years with an Immortal in Tangiers. Both of them had memories going back two millennia at least, both had met and lived with others of their kind many times over the centuries, and neither of them had ever met one who knew why they were the way they were, or indeed why none of them had ever had any children. "Just as well," Charles remembered Reinhardt joking as they lay in bed together smoking a heady mixture of hashish and opium. "Imagine if you ended up in bed with your great-great-great grandchild!"

Bridger took out his notebook. He sketched in a few more lines on the pencil portrait of Dulcie he'd been working on when Jessica had crossed the road, making him gasp, making him feel a brief sort of temporal vertigo.

He wrote a few more notes about the house, noting that it was still in the possession of the same family, then flicked back a few pages to his list of things he wanted to see in London before he moved on, and ticked off today's visit. Sometime in the next month or two, he'd go to the Long Laboratory in Switzerland, and deposit his notes and papers from this visit in his strongbox there. Then he closed the book, and tucked it back into his briefcase alongside the envelope with the photo in it. He was looking forward to seeing Lieutenant Donald Bridger's diaries later at the British Museum; after all, he hadn't seen them since he'd donated them back in 1780-something. He wondered how his handwriting had changed, noting that he could always compare it to the handwriting on the back of the photo of Benjamin, Dulcie and himself, taken outside 57 Church Road, Crystal Palace, London, in February 1930.

Marianne Taylor in Paris

One moment I was walking along Rue Hautefeuille at about ten o'clock on a cold, wet winter's evening, the next I was being bundled into an alley by three men. I let them push me against the wall, my mind's eye seeing how they saw me — a grey-haired woman in her sixties, her pearls and her handbag and her designer coat meant rich pickings. I saw the knife, long and sharp, come from under a black faux leather bomber jacket.

The guy in the middle, the one I reckoned to be the leader, was white, maybe twenty-three years old, tall, shaven-headed and powerfully built. He had, it had to be said, a beautiful face, with lusciously-lashed cornflower blue eyes, delicate, almost feminine lips smiling sweetly and a silver tooth glinting. Any other time, in a bar maybe, or a club, I'd have been into his pants like a shot; I'd have had a filthy dirty lost weekend with him, then left him drained, scratched and sobbing sometime on the Sunday afternoon.

"Come on darling," he said in French, "You know what we're here for, give us the goods, and we won't hurt you." There's no point in my describing the African boy and the Arab boy; they never spoke, in fact the only noises they made were groans and gurgles when I put them out of action less than a minute later. "Are we going to have to cause you physical pain, or are you going to hand over your handbag? Those pearls too, I'm sure we can get more than a few euros for them."

"I — I do not understand," I stammered, making my French sound a lot worse than it was. He giggled, an annoyingly high-pitched sound that made me revise how much I may have fancied him on any other day, and just how long I was going to put up with this merde before I disabled or killed him.

"Hand. It. Over," he said in English, glancing at my red leather handbag. I'd bought it just two weeks before in a very exclusive leather shop in Kyoto. He looked from side to side at his minions, and grinned more broadly, waggling the knife. "Now!"

"Non," I said. The smile faded slightly, and a perfectly formed eyebrow rose.

"No? No? I think you misunderstand me. You have five seconds to hand the bag and the pearls over, or I will stab one of your eyes."

"No," I said. "And if you try to do me any damage, your life will end almost immediately. Yours too," I addressed his minions.

His smile disappeared altogether now. He lowered his head slightly and thrust at my face with the knife.

It was a very poorly executed move, giving me plenty of time to weigh up my options. I could dodge to the left, drop, kick his feet from under him, then take the knife and drive it into his neck before his minions had stopped grinning; this is an easy enough move in decent footwear, but I had my Prada stiletto heeled boots on tonight, and was standing on wet cobblestones. I could also try swinging to the right, then kick him firmly in the groin with my left boot, and when he went down, drop onto the soft part of the back of his neck with the point of my elbow, ensuring unconsciousness within seconds; more iffy footwork though, and my thick coat might well absorb some of the blow.

I could even let him stab me in the eye; that worked a treat once in East London in the 1970s, the National Front goon who did it being aghast to see me take a step back, the knife still protruding from my eye socket, just before I gave him a straight fingered jab that smashed his windpipe so he dropped, choking to death, to the ground (once I got the knife out, the eye healed in less than a day, but it was very painful for the first hour or two). But I didn't want the pain and inconvenience of a burst eyeball, so I leaned left, grabbed his right arm with both hands, broke his wrist with a noisy, crunching twist, and pushed his own hand hard into his face, driving the knife up his nose and into his brain, stepping back sharply to avoid his blood. All this happened in maybe three seconds, so his friends had barely registered that he was falling to the ground before I turned to the one on the right, grabbed him by the face and smacked the back of his head viciously against an iron fire-escape frame. Then I spun and punched the third one between the eyes, pushed him over and stamped hard on his face.

And then, just what I didn't need, the whoop of a siren, a flashing blue light; les fucking gendarmes.

As a group, we Immortals keep our presence a secret; it's a hard and fast policy. We can't have mortals, with their century-at-best lifespans, knowing that we walk among them, we who've lived a couple of thousand years at least. For this reason, we don't advertise ourselves; we don't, for instance, stay in the same spot for hundreds of years, never ageing, always healthy and young; people would get suspicious. There was a time when that sort of thing could get one burnt at the stake, and that is a very, very painful way to go.

So, we age. Well, we appear to age. Over the space of sixty years, we'll appear to age sixty years; our hair goes grey or white, our faces become lined; occasionally a minor wound won't heal properly, leaving a scar. Basically, we appear to succumb to the sort of things that happen to mortals (we will, of course, still be completely fit and well, but we will appear frail and old, which makes being mugged a lot of fun). And every now and then, every sixty or so years, we up sticks and leave, we disappear, we walk away from whatever name, whatever situation we currently inhabit — sometimes we fake our own deaths — and we go and find ourselves somewhere quiet and safe, somewhere we won't be interrupted, and we nod off for a good month; we go into an incredibly deep Sleep — that's Sleep, not sleep. This is not much to do with refreshing mind and body. Well, yes, it is, but not in the simplistic nightly way it is for non-Immortals. During this time our bodies undo the greying and the ageing and the scars and the wrinkles and the lines, and we wake up a couple of kilos lighter, refreshed and full of energy and looking sixty years younger; sometimes our eyes change colour too. And we start a new life.

This is what I was organising when I got jumped. That afternoon I'd finalised the outright purchase of a small house with a deep cellar on the outskirts of Chatou, a rather nice town about ten kilometres outside Paris. The idea was to have the cellar fitted out, then Sleep in it, then live in the house for a decade or two under a new identity. I'd not been in Paris for longer than a couple of days since 1892 so it was about time I got back into its swing; I was fond of the place I'd first known, sometime in the fourth century AD, as Lutetia. I also had vague plans of renting out a lovely little pied-a-terre somewhere hip and cool in the middle of the city.

"Right, let's go over this yet again. Three street criminals, known to local police as having a history of violence, tried to mug you and, what, they fell out among themselves? One of them killed another by sticking a knife up his nose, then got his head kicked in by the third? And the third guy, can you tell me again what happened to him?" the capitaine asked. His name was Olivier Bluteau; he was a big black guy, with a tired, sympathetic manner, and I couldn't help but like him. He fiddled with a brass Zippo lighter, turning it over and over in his thick fingers, opening and closing it with that lovely distinctive clink. It was nearly two hours later, and this wasn't the first time we'd been through my story. I hadn't been charged, I was being interviewed 'under caution', but my coat and gloves and boots had been taken away and I had flimsy plastic sandals on my feet. Two cups of rubbish coffee stood on the table between us, untouched.

It had been explained to me that someone further down Rue Hautefeuille had seen the three men bundling me into the alley and flagged down a passing police car. Initially les flics came running up to me with guns drawn, but when they saw that all three of my attackers were out of action, that had confused the hell out of them. Another car arrived with Capitaine Bluteau five minutes later, then an ambulance, and soon the alley was filled with men in waterproof uniforms. I had been questioned in the car briefly, then brought here, to Commissariat de Police de la Gare Saint-Lazare. It had also been explained to me that one of the men, the leader, was dead, the one whose head I'd bashed against the fire escape was in a coma, and the other's jaw was so badly broken that he couldn't speak, plus his left retina was detached.

"Look, I don't know how many different ways I can tell you, I really don't know what happened," I said, laying on the 'little old lady' tone of voice heavily. "My eyesight isn't what it used to be, I'd taken my glasses off because it was raining, and it was dark in that alley. They started arguing, about what I don't know, they were speaking too fast for me to follow. Then there were thuds and crashes, one of them fell against me and I sort of got a lucky kick in, and next thing the police were there. It all happened very quickly."

"You 'sort of got a lucky kick in'? One of my officers says that as he pulled up in his car, he saw you stamp hard, with a stiletto heel, on the face of one of the three men who were lying on the ground in front of you, causing what we call 'life changing injuries'. Pretty lucky kick."

"Yes, pretty lucky kick. If I hadn't done that, who knows what he might have done to me?"

He looked at me for a long moment. I knew he didn't entirely believe me, but what could he do? He had a little old lady in front of him, and little old ladies don't tend to kill, maim or render unconscious fit young guys a third of their age.

"Yeah, who indeed," he said. "We have no witnesses, the nearest CCTV camera is around the corner, and Forensics are already using the word 'inconclusive'."

"Does this mean I can get my boots and gloves and coat back?"

"Not yet. I'm still waiting for—" And the door opened and a woman walked in. She was tall, and had very white skin, grey eyes and shoulder-length jet black hair. She appeared to be in her fifties, and wore a tired frown. Her face was handsome rather than beautiful, slightly androgynous, with sharp cheekbones and jawline, reminding me of a man I'd slept with in Tokyo, though her body was anything but mannish, seeming lush and curvy and womanly. She wore a dark grey jacket over a shimmery white blouse, with black trousers tucked into matt black calf length flat-heeled boots. Bluteau straightened in his chair and announced her arrival for the recording equipment. "Inspecteur General Duré has entered the room. Inspecteur?"

"Capitaine Bluteau, that will be all. Can we have the room please? I need to talk privately with Ms Taylor." Bluteau frowned, but he got up and left the room, announcing his departure to the tape; he was already pulling a tatty packet of Marlboro reds from his pocket. Ms Duré terminated the interview, turning the tape off, then sat down.

"Ms Taylor. Why are you in Paris?" she asked, in unaccented English.

"Is this official? You've turned the tape off. Do I have to answer?"

"No, no you don't. But it would make things much easier for you, and indeed for me, if you can answer some questions."

"Am I going to get arrested or charged?"

"No. You're not going to get arrested or charged with anything."

"Good. OK, the reason I'm in Paris is that I want to live here."

"Why?"

"Why not? It's a great city, and I've found a lovely little place just a few miles out of town."

"What is your name?"

"You know what my name is, it's Marianne Taylor."

"Is it?"

"Yes. You've presumably sent one of your gendarmes over to the hotel to get my passport by now."

"Yes, the Select Hotel on the Place de la Sorbonne." She opened the file she'd put on the table in front of her and took out my passport, opening it to the photo page. "Marianne Emily Taylor, born in January 1954 in London. Apparently."

"Apparently?"

"How old are you, Ms Taylor?"

A doubt flared in my mind. "What? What is this?"

"How old are you, Ms Taylor?"

"You can't work that out by looking at my passport?"

"How old are you, Ms Taylor?"

"Persistent, aren't you? OK, I'm sixty-two."

"Sixty-two what?"

"What?"

"You're sixty-two what?"

"You're confusing the hell out of me now. I'm sixty-two years old."

"Sixty-two years? Not decades?" And the penny dropped. But I went on with the bluff.

"Eh? You don't think I'd look a little older if I were six hundred and twenty years old?"

"No, Ms Taylor, I don't. And neither would I." And the penny dropped a little further.

"Ah, right, got you. How old are you, Inspecteur Duré?"

She smiled. "Call me Claire. I'm over two thousand years old, as far as I can tell. And so are you."

"Well, yes, uh, Claire. But… how did you know? I mean, that I was here."

"Because a) the whole building started buzzing with the story of how a small, sixty-two-year-old woman seemed to have seriously incapacitated three—" She paused, and took out an iPhone which was vibrating, read something off the screen, then continued, "seriously incapacitated three muggers. This made my antenna prick up. And b) when I walked down the corridor to this room, my Sense started to tingle—"

"Ah, you're one of those."

"Yes, I'm one of those. It's not a very long-range Sense, but it's pretty reliable."

I sighed. I'd met a few over the centuries, Immortals who had a sense of another one of us being nearby. The range varies, though it never seems to be more than about a hundred metres; a few can even tell the gender of the Immortal Sensed. By most reckonings, only about fifteen percent of us seem to have it, and it doesn't always work very well, but Ms Duré's seemed to be working just fine that night.

"Ok, yeah. So, what do you want to know?"

"What happened tonight?"

"Well, I got mugged, basically. They saw me, an elderly woman, walking alone late at night, they saw my coat and my handbag and my pearls and they thought 'easy pickings' and jumped me. So I killed the first guy, knocked out the second, and nearly kicked the third one's face clean off. Assholes. If it hadn't been for your lot showing up so fast, I would have just walked rapidly away, maybe calling Very Very Old in to send a clean-up squad. Actually, hang on, you're not VVO, are you?"

"No, I'm not VVO, though there is a branch in Paris. I meet with one of them occasionally, and I'm going to have to tell them about this. Also, the second mugger isn't unconscious, he's dead too, he died about ten minutes ago, in hospital. Brain haemorrhage." She waved the iPhone at me. "You killed two men tonight."

"Oops."

"Yeah, oops." She sighed, then exploded, quietly. "For fuck's sake, what were you thinking? You couldn't just give them all a hefty kick in the balls and run?"

"Well, yes, I suppose I… I wasn't really… Look, have you tried running in stilettos? On wet cobbles? If I'd tried to leg it, I would have gone over, and they would've been all over me like a—"

"You're an Immortal, for fuck's sake!" she snapped. "You've been fighting off attackers for two fucking millennia, couldn't you have been just a little bit more discreet?"

"Well yes, but—"

"Not only have you caused a serious problem for the police, but you may also have drawn unnecessary attention to us, to our type, to us Immortals." She rubbed her forehead, pinching the bridge of her nose. "Plus, you're giving me a rotten headache."

"What, literally?" She did appear to be in some pain.

"Yes, literally. The Sense sometimes does that. So I'd be quite happy if you just fucked off out of here, left Paris, left France, and didn't come back."

"But I've just bought a house. I can't just—"

"Yes, you can, and yes you will. I'm going to have to work long and hard into the night to make this go away. In house," she gestured around the room we were in. "I'm going to have to make it sound like some sort of intelligence thing, like you're some sort of spy whose identity we can't afford to make public, though Capitaine Bluteau is no pushover. Not to mention the families and associates of those dead guys, they'll be on a war footing. So I'm sure you'll understand if I ask you to do me, and yourself, a huge favour by taking this—" and she slid my passport across the table, "and checking out of that hotel and getting on the next plane anywhere. Kapish?"

"Yes, but what about my house? I've just finalised the papers today!"

"I don't care about your house, Ms Taylor. Find somewhere else to live, in another country, do the Sleep, change your identity again, sell the house on the internet, whatever, I don't care, so long as you don't come back to Paris for a good few decades. Got it?"

"Is there an alternative?"

"Yes. I'll make sure you're charged with manslaughter, and remanded to La Sante prison. Then I'll see that you're shuffled through the system for a few years, might be the mid-2020s by the time you get out. I know, you won't be in any danger, you probably wouldn't be convicted, but it'll be boring as hell."

I sighed. "Well, if you put it like that…"

"I do put it like that, I really, really do. Please, Ms Taylor, go. OK?"

I paused, for effect only, then picked up my passport. I assumed she'd have a flag on it with the French borders' agency, and if I hadn't left the country within a day or two, she'd have the resources to have me lifted. "Can I have my coat and boots please?"

She took out her iPhone again, called a number, muttered something into it, then hung up. "They're on their way," she said.

"Thanks. Can I ask you a question?"

"Go on."

"Most of us Immortals tend not to get into too visible a position. Why are you working here?"

"Well, I got to Paris in the eighties, as an alleged twenty-something. I never worked as an actual cop before, and I just decided to give it a try. Turned out I'm rather good at it. Got promoted almost before I knew it; now I've reached these dizzy heights. I'm responsible for hundreds of officers, running big investigations, working on policy, strategy and protocol. I like it, to be honest, I'm helping protect a city I've come to love." She paused, looked at the door, and lowered her voice. "I was at the Bataclan in November last year, went to see Eagles of Death Metal, had a night off, went by myself. I was there when it all kicked off, got shot in the arm. But I managed to grab the gun off the guy and shoot him in the face with it. Called for assistance on my cell. When RAID arrived—"

"RAID?"

"Recherche, Assistance, Intervention, Dissuasion," she said in French. "Elite armed response unit. When they arrived, I'd killed another one, he had an AK47 and three grenades. I'd stopped him before he could go into the ladies' toilets. There were a dozen people hiding in there. I joined them, and looked after them till RAID rescued us. No one knew I'd been shot, I told them I'd fallen in some blood, and it had healed by the following day. But it was horrible in there, and I'm very glad I was able to help, even a small bit." She paused again. "I sometimes think we have a responsibility to the mortals, to look out for them when evil comes calling. Have you never done something like that?"

"Oh yeah, a fair few times. Munich 1938, Moscow 1917. Not far from here in 1572, I saved a large family of Huguenots by killing a bunch of psychotic Catholics. I know what you mean."

"So, that's why I'm a flic," she said. "It kind of formalises it, and I'll do it till retirement in about ten years' time, then I'll do the Sleep, then I'll head off into the rest of the world again, and—" She was interrupted by a knock at the door. A young male officer came in with my coat and boots, gave them to me, then left. I put them on. "Well, it's been good meeting you," she said, "Even if you've caused me quite a headache."

"Literally and figuratively. Yes, good to meet you too. I'll go back to the hotel and try to get a flight somewhere as fast as I can. England maybe, I could always jump on the Eurostar. Haven't been to London since the seventies." I stood. She led me out of the interview room, and through a labyrinth of corridors and stairwells until suddenly we were in cold, damp night air on the pavement at the front of the building. We hugged. "Good luck with the, you know, crime guys," I said. "Sorry to have, well…"

"Au revoir," she said. "Rester hors des ennuis!" Then she turned and walked back into her fortress.

I was lucky enough to spot a cab almost immediately, and went back to the hotel, the unmarked police car following us not even trying to be discreet. At the hotel entrance I waited till the flics had found a spot to park before going inside, waving goodnight to them as I did. At the reception desk I was greeted coldly; they were not happy at having several wet gendarmes turn up to search my room and take my passport and I was informed that I was required to leave the following morning and never come back.

Up in my suite, I got my iPad out and booked a business class seat on the following day's mid-morning Eurostar to London, and a room at the Savoy. Then I showered and went to bed. Lying there in the semi-darkness, I fiddled with the tablet, trying to decide what I'd do once I got to London. The house in Chatou would have to go on the market, that was for sure. It was a real pity, I'd been looking forward to a few decades in a small, pretty town, beside a big, beautiful city. But it couldn't be helped. Maybe I could do the same in London, or maybe I could go further afield. I'd never, in my two thousand years, been in Ireland; I'd just never got round to it. I fired up another Safari page, and started browsing estate agents in some of the posher suburbs of Dublin.

Shane Tierney in Dublin

We Immortals are far more likely to survive serious, potentially life-threatening injury than non-Immortals, it's a given among our kind, so contact with mortal medics is kept to a minimum. Although our own scientists have never been able to find out why we are such tough motherfuckers, we can't rule out the chance discovery of our secret by one of theirs, their interest piqued by how suspiciously fast we're healing. So I wasn't best pleased to wake up in a hospital bed.

I cast my mind back. Breakfast in the hotel, a stroll around two museums followed by a solo lunch at a swanky restaurant in one of Dublin's posher bits, then the taxi to the suburbs, the meeting in the anonymous office in Dalkey, another taxi back into town... Ah, yes, that was it. The car had jerked violently sideways, I'd looked up from my phone to see the huge, slab-fronted juggernaut slamming into us, and after that... nothing. It had, it occurred to me, happened less than a mile from a hospital. Assuming that's where I was now, the ambulance had probably been there in minutes. I wondered what had happened to the cab driver, a dour North Dubliner with breath so bad I had to open my window. The truck had hit on his side, and I was sure he wasn't an Immortal like me.

The clock on the wall showed that it was just before five p.m., so I'd been out for about two hours. I wriggled and twisted in the bed, aches and pains registering themselves in my left shoulder, my face, and both legs. Sitting up was painful, but not impossible. I pulled off the blanket. There was a cannula in the crook of my left elbow; it wasn't attached to anything, though there was an unused drip stand nearby. I pulled it free, pushing some of the dressing against the wound as it bled a little. I realised as I did this that my left shoulder had some sort of tight, taped up strapping on it, and both lower legs were in big grey plastic casts with straps and Velcro all over them.

Shit, this wasn't good, it meant there were probably breaks; it meant I'd been x-rayed, something I really could do without. It was also going to make escaping quite difficult; if one or more bone was broken in each leg, it'd be late evening before I could walk, albeit gingerly, out of here. Nevertheless, I swung my legs out and let my feet fall to the floor, then stood. A very brief moment of dizziness cleared quickly. The healing process was obviously coming on well, because I was able to shuffle around the cubicle in a slow, unsteady circle.

I was wearing a standard hospital gown, white with a blue flowery pattern, and nothing else. On top of the locker by the bed, I saw my shoulder bag, and, in a plastic bin bag, my clothes, bloodstained, cut to bits. I pulled the iPad out of the bag, scraped some dried blood off the screen with a fingernail, then used its camera to check my appearance — not too bad, two swollen purple eye sockets, a shiny red nose, but nothing more than that. Still meant I wasn't going to be able to just get dressed and walk out of here. No taxi driver would pick me up from the front of the hospital if I looked like I'd just gone ten rounds with a combine harvester, and sooner or later, passing police would want to know what I was up to if I just walked back into town. And as for the hotel... No, I needed help. I went through the pockets of my ruined jeans and jacket, rescuing my iPhone and wallet. Then a voice said, "Mr Tierney! What on Earth are you doing?"

I was bundled briskly back into bed by a purse-lipped nurse who wouldn't listen to a word I was saying. The lack of cannula was noted and tutted about, and I was told, "Doctor will not be happy." I ignored him mostly, and as soon as he left the cubicle, I sat up, opened the iPad, and clicked the Very Very Old app. I logged in, going through the four-deep password process, skipped the social networking bits and clicked the link marked 'Heeeeeelp!'

Whoever built the app had a sense of humour. The next screen had a picture of a call centre drone yawning into his headset mic, with a speech bubble saying, 'What is your current registered name and the nature of your emergency?' I typed, 'Shane Tierney. In hospital, bad car crash, no clothes, need extraction soonest' into the box below it and waited. After a minute or so a text box popped up saying, 'Has your ID been compromised? How bad are your injuries? What age do you appear?' I answered, 'Called by name by nurse, must have seen cards in wallet so ID iffy. Both lower legs probably broken 3.5 hours ago, only proper injuries, though some facial bruising. Looking mid-40s'. Two minutes later, another text box popped up saying, 'Dublin VVO agent occupied, nearest agent in Belfast, can be with you in 90 mins. What hospital are you in?' I had seen the hospital's name on the nurse's name badge, so I answered, 'St Vincents', to which the answer, less than a minute later, was, 'See you soonish. Will appear as your sister Liz Tierney. What size clothes and shoes?' I let them know.

I'd just tucked the tablet away when the door opened and a woman in a white coat came in. Petite and pretty, she wore a scowl and seeing me sitting up on the edge of the bed with no cannula in my arm made her look even crosser. Her name badge said 'Dr Anna Kowalczyk'.

"Mr Tierney, isn't it?" A Polish accent. I toyed with the idea of answering in her native language, but decided that wouldn't be wise, given my desire to draw as little attention as possible to myself.

"Yes, Shane." I swung my legs back onto the bed.

"And it's Mr Tierney, not Dr Tierney, yes?"

"Erm, yes."

"So your medical knowledge is quite limited?" The sarcasm was strong in this one, I could tell.

"No, very little medical knowledge. But I am—"

"Then who told you that you could a) pull this out of your arm," she indicated the bloody cannula sitting on the bedside locker, "and b) get up and walk about on two broken legs? I hope they're hurting, I really do, that was not a clever thing to do."

"Actually, I need to get out of here as fast as I can, I have a really important meeting I have to—"

"A meeting? What on Earth are you talking about? Your left tibia and your right fibula both have greenstick fractures, you have a crushed lateral malleolus on your left leg, and you've torn the interosseous membrane in the right leg very badly. You've also torn your left trapezius. You shouldn't even be beginning to think about walking, and I'm pretty annoyed at you that you have. It's going to be several days before I can allow you to—"

"Look, this is a matter of life and death. I can't give you any details but—"

"Well then don't, because I wouldn't listen anyway. You have actually escaped serious injury in a very bad—"

"How did the cab driver do? Is he alive?"

She sighed. "No, he didn't make it, the chunk of metal that tore his neck open and hosed you down with his blood killed him in less than a minute. He was DOTS when the ambulance arrived.

"DOTS?"

"Dead On The Scene."

"And the truck driver?"

"A few scratches, concussion. You, on the other hand, were awake when the ambulance arrived, and trying to get your door open. The emergency guys had to use a spread cutter to get you out, but even then, you tried to stand up, they had to wrestle you onto a stretcher. Do you remember any of this?"

"Erm, no, sorry. But, look, I really really need to get going. My sister should be here soon, she's going to drive me to — well, I can't say. But I will be well looked after."

"What is it about 'You have two broken legs' that you don't understand? Yes, you were lucky, very lucky, to have escaped with nothing more, but you're still not out of the woods. I want you to go for more x-rays, we need to be absolutely sure there's no more damage higher up."

"No, no x-rays, I can't allow that." I didn't like the way this was going. I knew I was on dangerous ground here, but I really couldn't allow that to happen.

"You can't allow it? Why the... why not?"

"I don't... look I can't... look... I need to get out of here as fast as I can. I promise you I will be going directly to a damned good medical facility where I will be very well looked after indeed. But when Liz gets here—"

"Liz?"

"My sister. When she gets here, I will be getting dressed, and then I will be leaving. And I'm afraid you can't stop me."

"No, no I can't," she said angrily, "But I can express my opinion about this situation, and that is that you're making a fucking big mistake." She got up, and swished out of the cubicle; the door was too flimsy an affair to slam, but she still managed to shut it with an angry click.

A few minutes later another medic, this time a junior, came in with a clipboard, and started asking for information. They already had my alleged name, so I gave them one of my Dublin properties as my address, the twelfth of May 1972 as my date of birth, and my sister 'Liz Tierney' as my next of kin. They had been unable to ascertain my blood type, which he said was an unusual occurrence, but he didn't seem surprised when I refused to allow more blood to be taken. After a while, he left me to my own devices.

I spent the next hour messing about with the iPad, then a VVO message box pinged onto the screen. I opened it up with my passwords; it said, 'Liz Tierney is 20 mins away. Please have all your belongings ready to go, do not leave anything behind. We have a tracksuit, hoody, underwear, trainers and a beanie hat, all black, plus a burner mobile phone with two hours talk time on it. Please acknowledge receipt of this message'. I sent back 'Roger Wilco' then put everything in my bag and did up the zip.

At twenty to seven, after the briefest of knocks, the cubicle door opened, and a woman walked in saying loudly, "Shane! Darling brother, what have you done to yourself?"

She was one of those people over whom your glance passes, so anonymous did she look. She seemed about forty, had mousy hair in a cheap cut, off the peg glasses, a generic grey cotton suit, probably bought in a mid-range retail park and cheap flat black shoes. Her disguise was near perfect. It wasn't until one looked the third or fourth time that one realised how flawless her skin was, how beautiful her blue-grey eyes were, and that the haircut had been purposely badly pinned up. The glasses had clear, non-correcting lenses in them. I stood up as she closed the cubicle door. We spoke slightly louder than was necessary, for the benefit of any nosey listeners.

"Hi, Sis," I said. "Sorry to drag you away. But thanks for coming."

"That's OK, darling, what's a big sister for? Are you mobile?"

"No," I lied. "We'll need to borrow a wheelchair."

"I've got one outside the room. You get changed, and I'll bring it in. Here, I've brought you some clothes." She held out a big boxy paper bag, the sort one gets in department stores. I tipped it onto the bed, and tracksuit bottoms, a teeshirt, pants and socks, a hoody, a beanie and a pair of trainers fell out, all brand new, all black. She opened the cubicle door and grabbed a bog standard looking wheelchair from outside, and wheeled it in. She turned, closing the door, just as I took off the hospital gown, and stood naked in front of her. She looked me up and down, then hand-signed, "How mobile are you really?"

"A slow shuffle is all I can manage at the moment," I signed back, then sat on the edge of the bed to get dressed. The track suit trousers just about fit over the casts; the socks and trainers would have to be left off for the moment. In the hoody pocket was an old Samsung phone.

"OK, we'll use the wheelchair. The van is parked near the main entrance."

I signed, "Cool. What's your real name?"

"Harriet at the moment. Call me Harry."

"OK. How did you get here so quick?"

"Helicopter from Belfast to Baldonnell, picked up the hire van there. We'll go straight to your hotel. Which one is it?"

"The Merrion."

"Nice," she signed. "We'll talk more in the van. Now back to the sister-brother act."

"OK, looking good," Harry said a minute later as I pulled on the hoody and hat. "Let's get you into this wheelchair."

Dr Kowalczyk scowled at me as I signed myself out with an unreadable scrawl, then Harry wheeled me down a ramp to an anonymous looking black SUV. As we approached, the driver's door opened and a woman got out. She was black, slim, taller than me, looking to be in her sixties, and was dressed in a tight black leather catsuit, a chauffeur's peaked cap and Wayfarer sunglasses.

"This is Mimi," Harry said. "She's training as a VVO agent."

"Mimi, hi," I said as she slid the side door of the SUV open, and held out a hand to help me stand.

"Shane, hello. D'you know, I think we've met," she said as I climbed laboriously into the luxurious interior and did up my seat belt.

"Really? When?"

"Chicago, 1968. You helped me not get violently arrested."

"Erm, I don't… Oh! Hang on, during that Vietnam demo in the summer? That was you?" She smiled and nodded. "Wow. I never knew you were one of us! I wondered what became of you."

"That was me, I looked about twenty at the time, but you looked the same age as you do now." She turned to Harry. "I was getting my ass kicked by three white cops on a side street. This guy runs up, all cool and beatnicky and hepcat in his black poloneck and skinny black jeans, knocks one over and takes his gun, jams it in his mouth, and makes the other two drop me, and toss their guns. We then ran like fuck. You threw the gun in the river, yeah?"

"Yep."

"I knew what you were, I have the Sense, but before I could tell you I was Very Very Old too, we ran into that other riot, got split up, and I never saw you again." And she leaned into the car, and kissed me on the cheek. "Thanks, man, that was a good thing to do."

"Any time. I'm glad to hear you got out of there. I'd only gone to visit a friend who worked nearby, a non-Immortal, when it all kicked off. Saw a black woman getting a right beating off some white cops, so I couldn't help but wade in."

"Right you two," Harry interjected, smiling. "If you could just break up this tender reunion and remember who's the client and who's the driver — the trainee driver — we can get our asses moving, eh? Maybe later you can fuck."

"Is that part of the service too?" I laughed. "Excellent!"

As we pulled out onto Merrion Road, Harry opened a laptop and started tapping away at it.

"Right, I'm going to hack into the hospital's IT system, see if I can delete your records and x-rays. Don't want any more of a paper trail than is strictly necessary." She tapped away for a few minutes, then she humphed. "We have a problem," she said.

"We do?"

"Yep. It seems your Doctor Kowalczyk is suspicious about you. Shit, there's actually no point in my trying to delete you, it'd just make things more obvious. She's just this minute emailed a colleague, a David Smyth in St Thomas's in London. Hang on, I'll read it out: '"Have just had odd patient in A&E, male called Shane Tierney. He was in a very bad RTA, taxi driver DOTS. Tierney broke fibula in R leg, and tibia in L leg, yet walking in a couple of hours. Also, something odd at the top edge of one of his x-rays too, almost like…'" And here, Harry stopped, and turned to look at me, then went back to the screen. '"Almost like something attached to right femur just above knee, almost looks like jubilee clip. It's indistinct and shady, but he wouldn't let me do any more x-rays or bloods. He signed himself out fast as he could. Picked up by woman claimed to be sister though they looked nothing like each other and have different accents. Left just before the police came to talk about the accident. Reminded me of that conversation we had in Oxford about smuggling. I know what you're like for a medical mystery. Give me a ring as soon as you get this.'"

And she turned to me again and said, "What the fuck are you up to, Mr Tierney?"

"Seriously, Harry, don't go there. I can't say."

"Is it illegal?" said Mimi from the front.

"Please, I'm not going to…"

"For fuck's sake Shane," Harry said. "Do you want us to just push you out of the van? Leave you to make your own way home? Tell us what's going on or we'll do just that."

I sighed. "OK, I can tell you some of it. I sometimes have... a container attached to my right femur. It's about two hundred and eighty millimetres long and fifty-five millimetres in diameter. Technically, it's an endoprosthesis, it's made of a kind of high-tech living plastic that doesn't set security scanners off and my body doesn't try to reject it. I use it to transport... things in."

"Things?" Mimi said.

"Things."

"What sort of things?" Harry said.

"Small, very valuable things," I said. "I get them in by cutting my leg open, taking the container out, filling it, and putting it back in. Obviously, my leg heals really quickly, after a few days there's no scar. There are two small clips attached to my femur that the container gets slotted into, they're made of the same material. That must be what she saw."

"Clips! What the fuck?" Mimi exclaimed.

At the same time Harry said, "Jesus H Christ! What's in there at the moment?"

"Nothing," I said.

"Stop the car!" Harry shouted. "Stop the fucking car!" Mimi pulled over, much to the annoyance of some guy in a Beemer, and stopped at the kerb. Harry slid the door open.

"Out!" she yelled "Get out of this car!"

"What the fuck?" I said.

"Seriously, if you don't tell me what's in your fucking… internal saddle bag, I will dump you here and now, and fuck off into the sunset."

"Whaaat? You're joking! You're supposed to be helping me!"

"I'm supposed to be helping extract you from a difficult situation, not helping you with some sort of dodgy criminal activity. Seriously, you have three seconds, or it's fucking pavement time. What is in there?" She hissed, thumping me on the thigh in emphasis.

I sighed. "OK, but before I tell you, it's not as illegal as it sounds."

"What's in there?"

"Nothing, the cylinder isn't in there at the moment, just the mounting clips. But until four days ago, it was there, with a Caravaggio in it."

"A… a what?" Harry said.

"A Caravaggio. A drawing by Caravaggio."

"Caravaggio? You mean Michelangelo Merisi da Caravaggio, Italian painter of the sixteenth and seventeenth century?" Harry and I looked at Mimi, who was peering back between the front seats.

"Yes, that's exactly who I mean. It was rolled up," I said.

"And where did you get it?" Harry asked.

"Do I get to plead the fifth on this one?"

"Fuck off. Where did you get it? And when?"

"From a guy in Italy, couple of weeks ago. I can't tell you his name because I was never introduced to him. He wasn't one of us."

"And who put it into your leg?"

"Another guy in Italy, he was one of us."

"And it was taken out four days ago."

"Yeah. I was coming back from the pay-off in Dalkey when I had the crash."

"So you have a large wad of currency about your person?"

"No, it was done by transfer."

There was silence for a few seconds, then Mimi spoke.

"Which Caravaggio was it?" she asked.

"You won't have heard of it."

"Try me."

"*Girl Eating a Peach*, it's called. It looks like she's about to suck a cock."

"He was a dirty bugger, was Caravaggio. But yeah, you're right, I've never heard of it. I did a history of art degree in the eighties, got a first, specialised in Italy, why have I never heard of it?"

"Because it was never made public, he made it as payment for someone he owed money."

"An unknown Caravaggio? That'd be, well, priceless."

"And it was in your leg why?" Harry asked.

"Can we get moving please? I'd like to get back to the hotel and lie down for a bit. My legs are killing me."

Harry nodded, and Mimi pulled out into the traffic again, this time annoying someone in an Audi.

"So what was this Caravaggio doing in your leg?"

"It got stolen from its owner, I was part of the team that got it back for him; some professional did the actual thieving, I did the carrying. It's not priceless to him, just of huge sentimental value."

"Ah, it was one of our lot," Mimi said.

"Yeah, it was one of our lot. It had to be got from Milan to Dublin very discreetly, so I was hired to do the courier work, the guy it was stolen back from has people everywhere. I got paid a third up front, a third after the removal, which was in my hotel bathroom four days ago, and a third today after the picture had been reunited with its owner and verified. So, no real crime was committed and you haven't besmirched the good name of Very Very Old by helping facilitate any kind of criminal activity."

Harry snorted. "No, you're just being a massive pain in the arse. I bet you got fucking well paid for this too."

"Yes, I did," I said. "But… look, you're VVO, right?"

"Obvs."

"Do you have to, you know, include all these details when you report back to HQ?"

"Yeah, we kind of do."

"Shit, I thought as much. They're going to be pissed at me, aren't they?"

"Yep."

"Much I can do about it?"

"Duh, stop fucking doing it. You've had a close call VVO are going to have to be aware of today. So no more, OK?"

"OK," I kind of lied. "But, look, can we just shut up about the whole thing? I'm tired, I'm in pain, and I need a soft horizontal surface and a huge whiskey. Have you got any recreational narcotics? Dope, coke, Es? No, what am I saying, of course you haven't."

"Yes, you're absolutely right. Now, shut up for a bit, I need to organise the next bit as fast as I can." She took out an iPhone.

"The next bit? Surely we just pick up my kit and go to the airport?"

"No," she sighed, "I can't sanction leaving Ireland by conventional means. You, as Shane Tierney, won't be flying anywhere in the near future. It sounds like either you and your saddle bag have been spotted by the medical profession before, possibly by this Smyth guy—"

"Well, it's possible I suppose. But is it that big a risk?"—

"Of course it fucking is! One of our raisons d'être is that the mortals have no idea of our existence, as well you know. And so far, for the last two thousand or more years at least, we've done just fine at keeping it that way. We do not want it to all go spectacularly tits up just because of you and your poxy saddle bag. So, one, we need to get you discreetly out of the country, retiring your Shane Tierney ID as we do, and two, we need to investigate, very, very carefully indeed, both your Dr Kowalczyk and this Smyth guy in London." She sighed. "But first, let's get you back to your hotel, pick up all your stuff and... I'm assuming your passport is there?"

"Yeah."

"And get you the hell out of Ireland."

"If not by air, then how?"

"We're on an island, how do you think?"

"Duh. By sea."

"Obvs."

By the time Mimi was helping me hobble into the lift in the hotel's lobby, Harry was looking a hell of a lot more relaxed. She'd had two brief conversations on her mobile, and had reported that things were coming together.

In my suite, I lay down on the bed, Harry slumped on the sofa, and Mimi hit the minibar. She made me a huge whiskey and soda, Harry a long G&T, and poured herself a pint of Prosecco. We clinked glasses, then all drank together, all sighed together, then all burst out laughing together.

"So what's the next step?" Mimi asked.

"We're getting this guy onto a boat from Dun Laoghaire at six a.m.," Harry answered.

"A boat? I thought the ferries didn't sail from there any more," I said.

"Who said anything about ferries?"

"Oh. So we've got, what, about ten hours to kill."

"Yep," said Harry. Then she smiled. "Anyone fancy a fuck?" She started to unbutton her blouse, revealing cleavage and a hint of snowy white bra.

"So it is part of the service!" I laughed. "Excellent!"

An hour later, in a slowly cooling intimately entwined heap on the bed, we three lay naked, talking about old times. Very old times.

When two or more Immortals are finished with the business at hand, be it a VVO extraction, or an enthusiastic three way fuck, their conversation often falls into one of four intertwined subjects; what we are, why we're like we are, why we can't reproduce and how many of us have been killed.

"Aliens," I said.

"Homo Sapiens Mark 1.1" Harry said.

"Humans enhanced by aliens," Mimi said.

And:

"So we can infiltrate Earth," I said.

"Evolution," Harry said.

"Shits and giggles," Mimi said.

And:

"You'd run a serious risk of hooking up with your own great grandkid and having sex with them. It'd fuck up the gene pool hugely," Mimi said.

"Agreed," Harry said.

"Agreed," I said.

As to the last, how many of us have been killed, well, that was somewhat more serious. Yes, as I had demonstrated that very day, we are tough motherfuckers, and can easily take the sort of damage non-Immortals would be killed by, but we're still not entirely indestructible. We each related the tale of one Immortal who'd turned out not to be.

"I knew a guy in Prague back in the 1400s, guy called Jan Huss," I said. "He was an interesting guy. Not especially likeable, but intelligent and witty. A reformer before Martin Luther was even thought of; he had a real hard on about Papal Indulgences, and he spoke out against them. So of course the Catholic Church lifted him, did all the usual things they did in the name of the love of God, limbs all smashed up, various bits and pieces pulled off with red hot pliers, and so on. But he refused to recant, so they burnt him at the stake. They had to chain him to it by the neck, because he couldn't stand. I can still hear the screams. It took him a long, long time to die, and in a huge amount of pain. Poor fucker."

"Shit, what a way to go," Mimi said, her hand loosely cupping my balls. Harry was tucked in behind her.

"Didn't do the Church any favours either, it kicked off the Hussite Wars in Bohemia, sowed the seeds of the Reformation. What about you?"

"An execution too," Mimi said, "Paris 1792. He was a highwayman, got caught by a dozen soldiers after mugging someone. He was executed a couple of months later, first person ever to be guillotined. I Sensed him from a side street, but he was guillotined as I arrived in the Place de Grève, just too late to save him. Saw the head land on the ground, they hadn't added the basket to catch it yet, and our eyes met. I swear he was still there for another few seconds before some fucker picked up his head and started waving it around.

"Fucking hell."

"Yeah. Harry?"

"London. The Blitz. A direct hit with an incendiary." She closed her eyes. "She was a good woman, was Clarice."

There was a minute's silence. Then Mimi sat up, picked up her empty glass, and said, "The tide's gone out. Barkeep, a refill please."

And later still, showered and clothed, eating sandwiches and drinking coffee and tea sent up by room service, Mimi and Harry quizzed me more about the 'saddle bag'. I had decided I liked the name.

"When did you first have it fitted?" Mimi asked.

"About three years ago. A friend, a Very Very Old friend, needed some... some things, some small, incredibly valuable things moved discreetly from one place to another, without bothering the authorities as to their existence, and a drunken conversation came up with the idea of hiding them internally. Kind of like those poor bastards who swallow a condom full of coke and fly from Peru to Heathrow, only with our own special twist. He knew a surgeon, we both knew a research implant specialist, we concocted the whole thing over dinner at Le Gavroche."

"And you just… cut yourself open and shove it in?" Harry said with a frown.

"I don't do the cutting, I have a couple of surgeon friends scattered around Europe who can do it for me, and it has to be positioned very carefully, hence the clips, but essentially, yes."

"Does it hurt?"

"Once it's in position, not much. It makes me walk with a bit of a limp, and you can see that my right thigh is slightly fatter than my left when I've got it in."

"Ew," said Mimi. "I think I'd rather stick it up my arse."

"It does take a bit of getting used to. But bear in mind, I only do two or three trips a year, and it's only ever in for a few days. The next trip's not till January, probably."

"What will be in it then?" Harry asked. I whistled and looked at the ceiling.

"So where's the saddle bag now?" Mimi said.

"Somewhere in Wicklow. It'll get posted back to my place in London in a few days. I have three of them. When I get it back, it gets sterilised and packed away in a very safe place."

"I'm impressed and disgusted in equal parts," said Harry.

"Thanks, almost," I said.

We left the hotel at five a.m., the desk charging me extra for my two guests; the night manager's sneers were barely contained. I paid in cash. We climbed into the SUV, and drove swiftly through the empty streets, barely speaking. I had taken off the plastic casts, and put on socks and trainers; my legs were in pretty good shape now, though covered in yellowing bruises; my shoulder was fine, and my face was almost back to normal.

At Dun Laoghaire Harbour, we drove out onto the old Coal Pier. At the end, Mimi pulled over and we all I climbed out.

"There's your ride," Harry said, and pointed to a decent-sized cabin cruiser moored by the steps. An anonymous looking bloke in a black bomber jacket and beanie hat was standing in the cockpit looking bored, smoking, fiddling with his phone. "He'll take you to Liverpool. It'll take a few hours."

"Is he one of us?"

"No, he thinks we're just bog-standard criminals. We use him and his family sometimes, he asks no questions beyond 'what time' and 'how far'. You're just a body. So to speak."

I hugged and kissed both women, Mimi slipping a piece of paper into my hoody pocket as I did and briefly licking my lips.

"Thank you both for everything you've done," I said. Mimi touched her hat's peak with a forefinger.

Harry said, "Just make sure to give us five stars on the app," with a smile.

An hour later, I went out onto the deck, and after putting a lead diving weight into it, I dropped my bag overboard: passport, bloody clothes, bank and credit cards, iPhone, iPad and all. Aside from my favourite pair of Occhiali sunglasses, all I had with me now were the cheap, generic clothes I stood up in, the burner mobile, and a wallet full of cash. I wouldn't be landing anywhere official when we got to the UK. My plan was to buy a train ticket to London. Then I rooted in the hoody's pocket and pulled out the bit of paper Mimi had given me. It just had a mobile phone number on it, a British one. I smiled, tucked it back into my pocket, and went back below.

Patrick Smith in New York

About a fortnight after I'd buried my eighty-first wife, a friend — a Very Very Old friend — showed up on my doorstep.

I was sitting on the roof terrace with a lunchtime salad, spring sunshine bathing me warmly, trying to decide what to do next. When the iPad on the table chimed, and the app popped up with the entry phone screen, I jumped slightly, then peered at the face on it. I knew the face, I knew it well, but the only name I knew it by was probably way out of date. I tapped the speaker icon. "Spiros? Spiros Papodopolous? Is that you?" I said.

"Hello Patrick Smith! Or should I say Jake Wainwright? Have you ever danced with the devil in the pale moonlight?"

We sat on the terrace, a bottle of Prosecco between us. We hadn't seen one another in a hundred and twenty-eight years.

"I always hated it that that bloody film stole our line," Spiros said. He was looking well; he'd clearly Slept recently, and was sporting the body and looks of a handsome young man in his mid-twenties. His eyes, deep brown last time I saw him, were now a light golden hazel, but his hair was still jet black.

"Yeah, I know what you mean, I thought we'd invented it in 1880-something. Annoyed the hell out of me when I saw it." I sipped my wine. "So, what brings you here? And, well, what's your name these days?"

"Jamie. Jamie O'Brien. I was in LA the other day, and got to thinking about you, so I went to www.veryveryold.com and there you were, Jake Wainwright/Patrick Smith. Did you not get my message?"

"No, I only check in once or twice a month. I'm not madly computer orientated, to be honest, but I thought I should set up a profile, in case a Very Very Old friend came calling.".

"I'm glad you did. But then I saw the thing about your wife on a few news sites too. I'm so sorry for your loss, Patrick. I do call you Patrick now, don't I?"

"Yeah, no one knows me as Jake here. Thing is, I've lost lots of loved ones over the centuries, but it never gets any easier."

"And it was cancer?"

"Yep. Breast cancer initially, she beat that about eight years ago, then it came back last October, pancreatic, so she went quite quickly. Heart-breaking to watch."

"Oh man, I'm so sorry."

"Yeah. I guess it's why so few of us settle down with mortals, we're always the bereaved one."

"You always were the serial monogamist though, weren't you? Do you still swing both ways?"

"Technically yeah, but I haven't since we got married, a wedding vow is a wedding vow."

"And you ran this kids' foster home together?"

"Saint Nick's? Yeah, I can't have kids obviously, but Elsa couldn't either. So I bought the building over on Prince Street and we ended up with lots and lots of kids, it's one of the biggest foster homes in New York State. We take them in at all sorts of ages, from all sorts of backgrounds, and give them love and security and stability, we've had hundreds through our doors. We've got a superb education department, and some gifted social work people. Also helps that I qualified as a paediatrician in the seventies. But then Elsa and I retired, sort of, in 2003, though we still keep… kept in touch with the place, popping by most weeks."

"Wow, that's amazing. I'm full of admiration for the two of you. Why is it called Saint Nick's?"

"Saint Nicholas is the patron saint of New York, plus the kids loved the whole Christmas connection."

"Ah, cool." He lit a cigarette. "So what are you going to do next?"

"To be honest, I don't know. I should really Sleep and move on, I can't stay here much longer. I mean, look at me. I am, according to my passport, eighty-three."

"Looking very good for it though," Jamie grinned. "When did you last Sleep?"

"1953."

"Jesus, that's a long time ago."

"Yeah, but when Elsa and I met I was, allegedly, already nearly forty. And we fell in love, and we got married and settled down together and then ten years later there was Saint Nick's and so forth. So I couldn't really disappear for a few weeks, then reappear as my younger self, could I? Obviously, I never told Elsa what I was, I invented a pretty boring life up to then, didn't refer to it a lot." I took one of his cigarettes and lit it. "The thing is, I like this life, I like this bit of New York, and I still love living here."

"It is a good part of town, I'll give you that. Didn't David Bowie live around here?"

I stood up, and walked over to the eastern side of the terrace, overlooking Lafayette Street. "Come over here." Jamie joined me. "See that roof terrace over there, the one with the olive trees?"

"Is that his place?"

"Yeah. I still see Iman out there sometimes. She walks down to Whole Foods Market on her own too, no minder or anything, and people give her space. She and Bowie used to walk their little dogs around the block every day, and people left them alone then too. It's one of the many things I like about this area. I spoke to him a few times in the Irish pub down the road, he used to pop across for a pint every now and then. Nice bloke. Plus, he gave us tickets for one of his shows to put in a raffle at Saint Nick's, which was very kind of him. I was very sad when he died, this whole area was. Ever see him live?"

"Couple of times, I always liked him. I met him too, in Berlin in the seventies, I owned an electronics company, we did some fitting out for Hansa. Yeah, he was a good man."

Later, after night had fallen, I made dinner — lobster ravioli prepared from scratch, with a tomato and curry leaf broth. In the afternoon, we'd popped out for a couple of pints at The Crooked Tree over on St Marks Place, then taken a circuitous route back via a good fishmonger for the shellfish, and Essex Street Market for the vegetables.

"Man, this place is up itself!" Jamie hissed.

"Sssh!" I whispered back, trying not to giggle. I walked us past Saint Nick's too, though we didn't go in. Iman had nodded to me as we passed her on Prince Street.

"Wow," Jamie said as he tucked in "You can still cook!"

"Thanks man. It's something I still love doing after all these years."

"Ever think about running a restaurant again?" We'd run a very successful place in Lille in the nineteenth century, selling it as a going concern when we 'retired' and Slept and went our separate ways in 1888.

"Too much like hard work. You?"

"God no, these days I'm in online security and web development. I worked with IBM in the seventies, and Tim Berners-Lee in the nineties. Top man, Tim, as it happens, a very very clever guy."

"What, you invented the internet? I'm impressed."

"Nah, that was definitely Tim. Well, mostly. But I did help with the hardware side of it. Gotta say, the digital age has helped us lot keep in touch way more easily. I've done some online stuff for VVO too, though I've never been an agent," he said, and sipped his Marsanne. "But look, are you serious about not wanting to move on? Do you really want to stay here?"

"Yeah, I do, I really do, it's my home. Why?"

"I never really did it that way. I've always moved on. I mean, you'd have to come back as, I don't know a grandson or something, some sort of family connection maybe. And it'd take a certain amount of acting too. You can't have anyone know who you really are, obvs."

"I don't mind that, I've done it once or twice before. Scott City in Kansas in the 1700s, I left town in my eighties, and came back six months later as my own grandson, with a message to say my grandaddy had died." I exaggerated a Kansas accent. "Had to pretend not to know the town for a while, but I ended up staying there thirty years. Married a girl whose grandmother had been one of my old flames."

"I'm sure it's doable," Jamie said. "I can help you with the computery side of it if you like."

"OK, I'll start thinking about it."

So Jamie rented a small apartment down the street a few days later, installed a top-of-the-range PC in the sitting room, and got to work, hacking into government systems in the US, the UK and Sweden, setting up IDs and legends for a fictitious brother and sister-in-law of mine who lived in Sweden, and their alleged daughter, son-in-law and grandson. Soon, Jamie got a job as an IT administrator for Saint Nick's; Jeff, our usual guy, had been making want-to-go-travelling noises for some time now, so I made him the gift of a round-the-world air ticket for his fortieth birthday, and he shot off as fast as he could.

I started seeing more of Saint Nick's over the next couple of months; as a bereaved husband, it was expected of me by the staff there, and they showed me nothing but kindness. I did feel slightly guilty about the lies I would soon be telling them, but I tempered that with the fact that it was for the very best of motives. I had no more contact with Jamie than any director would have with the new IT guy.

Then in October, I announced my retirement again. On the first Saturday that month, I threw a party in Saint Nicks' main hall, with buffet tables catered by Whole Foods, wine from the quirky little place run by the English guy on Bowery, beer from the warehouse on Christie, and music by a local rock covers band. Later, there'd be a disco DJed by Moby, who owed me a favour. But before the dessert was done, I stood up, ting-

tinged my wine glass with a spoon, and waited till the hubbub of chat and laughter died away.

"Good evening, folks," I said "And thanks for coming. It's great to see so many familiar faces, it's nice to feel appreciated."

"Who are you again?" Samuel, our financial controller and wannabe comedian, called out. "I just came for the food!" There was scattered laughter.

"Hey, I hope you found the kosher table Sam, or I'll tell your Mom!" I quipped back, to a much bigger laugh. "But seriously folks, I need to let you know of a few things. One is something the more eagle eyed among you will have spotted, and that is that this is my second retirement party. The first was thirteen years ago, when Elsa and I officially retired from the day-to-day running of Saint Nick's. Sadly, she died back in March, I kind of came back here to, well, my family, and, it was like I'd never left. But now it's kind of time to leave again, and this time for good. And not just leaving Saint Nick's, but New York. I'm taking off on my travels, I've got a bucket list of stuff to see and do around the world, and by God, over the next few years, I'm going to do it. You know, the Taj Mahal, Machu Picchu, Sydney Opera House, all those things we're supposed to get to see at least once in a lifetime. My ticket is booked, and I leave next Saturday, first stop London England. Might even drop in to Buckingham Palace and say hello to the Queen!" Scattered laughs. "I'll be in touch, from time to time, postcards or whatever... Do they still do postcards? And maybe even the occasional email. Meanwhile, I know the current directors are doing a terrific job, so I see no reason at all to change how the place is run. The Trust owns it, I haven't since the late nineties, so the only real difference you'll see here will be a little less of me complaining about the coffee. For now though, I'd like everyone to raise their glasses, and drink a toast…" Glasses lifted all over the hall "… to St Nicholas's Foster Home for Children, New York."

"To St Nicholas's Foster Home for Children, New York," echoed every voice in the room. In a far corner I could see Jamie O'Brien grinning from ear to ear as he drank deep of the Prosecco.

"Right, back to the desserts," I said. "In about half an hour the band will be on, and after that, a disco with a very special surprise guest!" There was a round of applause as I sat down, then I stood again, and it died away as I waved my hands in the air. "Whoops, nearly forgot, there is one more thing; my great-nephew, a kid by the name of Jake Wainwright, will be interning here in a month or two, probably for six months or so. The Trust have been told all about him, and they're cool with him being here. He's my brother's daughter's son, and he's bright and eager, and he loves New York. He's also lucky enough to look very like I did when I was that age!" Laughter. "So show him how tough working here can be, but be nice to him too, he is, like I say, a good kid. Um, I think that's it," I said, and sat down again.

And after that, it was a simple matter of signing my apartment over to 'Jake Wainwright', tidying up a few last bits and pieces, and heading off into the world. The night before I flew to England, Jamie came over, and I cooked a late supper, after which we took our drinks out onto the terrace and lit cigarettes. Later, in bed, snuggled up together, we talked of the near future.

"Looking forward to being 'Jake' again then?" Jamie said.

"I am, I really am. Though killing off Patrick Smith is going to have to be done very carefully. He'll need to disappear in some sort of sailing accident, I think, so the body is never found. His alleged brother will let Jake know, then I'll tell Saint Nick's. I'll also need to handle being there as a noob carefully. And CUNY too." I'd enrolled Jake Wainwright on a social work degree course at City University of New York. "Then my eye might be caught by the devilishly handsome IT guy at Saint Nick's…"

"About time too!" Jamie laughed. "You know David in the back office has been chatting me up something rotten?"

"David? Wow, I never even knew he was gay! I'd better get a move on!"

Two days later, I lay down on a bunk bed in the locked cellar of another very very old friend's house, one in a small, anonymous dormitory suburb in the South of England, and started the series of chants and mental exercises that sent me into a deep, deep Sleep…

Shirley Mitford in Tokyo

Flight JL7017 out of LAX passes easily. I watch a couple of films and TV shows, play some games on my tablet, eat two rather good meals and drink a lot of champagne. Initially, the steward in first class seems wary of allowing me to drink so much, especially given that I appear to be a woman in her seventies. But when he sees it having no discernible effect on me, he gives in and keeps them coming. By the time we touch down in Tokyo eleven hours later, I've had eight bottles of Cristal and earned his undying admiration.

The limo driver clearly approves of my destination, Ginza Conrad Six, one of the most prestigious buildings in the city. One of my tech companies leases a penthouse apartment there from one of my real estate companies; it's a mid-sized duplex with sitting room, dining room and kitchen downstairs, and two bedrooms and a ridiculously luxurious bathroom above, on the fifty-first floor of the building, over two hundred metres above street level. It's comfortable and, situated on the North East corner of the building, it has a great view. More importantly, it's incredibly secure, with its own lift and two passcoded security doors just to get to its lobby. My company has been using it since the building first went up in the late nineties, though I've only stayed here a handful of times. It's up here that I plan to Sleep, for the first time since the late sixties. But there's something else I need to do first.

I was in Japan on the eleventh of March, 2011, as Shirley Mitford, an American woman in her early seventies. On that day, I was in Orikawa, a rather lovely little town in Miyagi Prefecture, about four hundred kilometres north of Tokyo, visiting a Very Very Old friend called Hiro Watanabe; I'd been there a few days. He also appeared to be in his seventies, though was showing no signs of wanting to retire from running the town's best izakaya, a bar/cafe/restaurant.

When the earthquake struck, I was alone on the tiny patio behind his house, drinking Asahi beer and flicking through a local newspaper. Hiro had driven down to the izakaya to fill a box with food and drink earlier; the plan was for him to collect me and drive me up into the hills over the town for a picnic. He said there were some spectacular views from up there. I wondered if it was too cold for some après lunch al fresco sex too. Our nightly romps in his bedroom had been a lot of fun, but there's nothing quite like doing it sky-clad.

I had experienced earthquakes before of course, many times. This one was middling to bad, the ground rumbling and shaking, with a sharp, violent shock every few minutes.

The ghastly wail of the tsunami loudspeakers kicked in twenty minutes later, with a five-minute warning of mild to mid strength tsunami — everyone to evacuate to higher ground immediately; the town was, after all, right on the coast. I had tried to ring Hiro's cell phone as soon as I felt the first tremor, and several times since, but it went straight to voicemail every time.

The reality was that the sheer size of the wave was underestimated, and it struck faster and harder than anyone expected. It hit Orikawa very quickly indeed. I've subsequently read that the wave rolled over the land at speeds in excess of eighty kilometres per hour. Certainly, when it came roaring up the hill Hiro's home was on, I couldn't outrun it. In my mind's eye, I can see it charging malevolently towards me, a black, roiling mess of filthy, lumpy water, the ruined remains of bits of house caught up in it, limbs torn from trees, a dog, a fridge, a motorbike, and, visible for just a second, a body, a human body. Then I was inundated.

The next hour or so is almost entirely blank in my memory. I can, of course, hold my breath for upwards of half an hour, so I assume that's what I did repeatedly, letting it wash me along, trying to minimise any damage done to me. Awareness returned to find me up a tree, a good couple of kilometres away from Hiro's. Another woman and two men were with me, all of us clinging on for dear life as, finally, the waters started to recede. I was covered in cuts and bruises, my left eye was closed, my nose and right arm were broken, and I was completely naked, save for a stopped wristwatch.

I stayed in Orikawa for a week after the tsunami, healing fast, and helping with the relief efforts, cooking rice and vegetables in the Buddhist temple at the top of the hill and looking for Hiro; I have the Sense, I can tell when there's another Immortal nearby, yet it didn't so much as twitch. The nearest I came to finding out what happened to him was when his car turned up in the car park by the harbour under a trawler, crushed flat; there was no sign of him in it. At the end of that week, I went back to Tokyo, spent a night in the apartment in Ginza, then flew back to LA and threw myself into my architectural practice.

I never saw Hiro again.

Today is the tenth of March; tomorrow is the fifth anniversary of the tsunami. After lunch in a department store food court in Tokyo's central railway station, I take a Nozomi Shinkansen to Sendai, an Express to Ishinomaki and finally a local bus to Orikawa, arriving a little before five o'clock. Haruto Hinata is waiting for me at the bus station, as planned. He's holding up a sign that says 'Shararee Mitoforodo' in Japanese. I've never met him before, though we have communicated through the online forums that sprang up soon after the tsunami, and Hiro, our mutual friend, had mentioned him occasionally. Haruto was in Osaka when the tsunami struck, and didn't make it back to Orikawa till after I left. He's in his sixties, non-Immortal, a tall, stooped man with a long face that wears a lugubrious, hangdog expression. He's in a baggy black cotton suit, open-necked white shirt and a black straw trilby. We shake hands.

"My car is in the car park. It is a ten-minute drive to my home," he says in heavily accented English.

"Excellent, and thank you very much for coming to meet me," I say in flawless, unaccented Japanese.

He smiles briefly. "Your Japanese is very good," he says, reverting to his native tongue. "Better than my English." He shows me to a small Nissan runabout, puts my overnight bag on the back seat, and we climb in.

He doesn't say much; it's a trait of people from Sendai. When I messaged him a few weeks ago, suggesting this trip, connecting it with the planned memorial ceremony in the town, even his text response was brief — 'I think that is good idea. You stay at my house. SMS me arrival time Orikawa'.

Hiro's izakaya is no longer there. The entire street it was on is no longer there. Well, the roadway is, mostly, pitted and scarred. But the buildings, low level timber ones for the most part, were swept away by the tsunami. I shed a very brief tear while Haruto looks away, then we move on.

Haruto's house is a modest, white, two-storey building near the top of a hill, with a commanding view over the town. Haruto parks on the street, and shows me in. His house is a triumph of miniaturisation; the front door opens straight into a small, well-appointed kitchen where we take our shoes off, and a sitting room beyond it has just enough room for a sofa, a small dining table with two chairs and a well-stocked bookshelf. A steep staircase leads up to two bedrooms, both four tatami mat-sized, and a miniscule bathroom with a shower cubicle and toilet. There is a balcony that wraps around two sides of the upper storey, both bedrooms having access to it. Despite its modest size, it's light and bright and airy, the skylight at the stop of the stairs helping. Haruto puts my bag on the futon I'll be sleeping on tonight, then we come back downstairs and he puts the kettle on.

"Tomorrow, would you like me to, ah, escort you to the memorial ceremony?" Haruto asks as we sit down with glasses of green tea.

"Yes please. Can I take you for lunch somewhere beforehand?"

"That would be very nice of you. Thank you," he says. He lapses into silence, his face stony. I don't want to talk; if I do, it will be about Hiro, and I will probably cry. Haruto is clearly a compassionate man, but like most Japanese people, he's careful with his emotional displays, so I don't want to do anything to upset him more than he already is. I try to think of something I can displace the sadness with. As if reading my mind, his hand falls on a black lacquered box, sitting on a shelf by the TV.

"Do you play Go?" he asks. I nod, and he opens the box. We play many games, we say very little. He beats me almost every time, despite the fact that I've been playing it for hundreds of years.

Later, I offer to make dinner for both of us, having noticed that Haruto's kitchen is stocked solely with ready meals. I go to a 7-Eleven down the road and buy ingredients for shabu shabu. After we've eaten, I go for a walk while Haruto washes up. I stop at the 7-Eleven again and buy a litre bottle of saké, then walk a couple of kilometres before stopping on the little green we passed on the way from the bus station. I sit on a bench, open the saké, and take a huge swig.

I wish I could get drunk. It looks like a lot of fun. Most of us Immortals can. But I'm immune to the effects of alcohol. One or two other Immortals I've met over the centuries are too; some don't respond to narcotics. I do, as it happens, I just don't like them much, those that I've tried. But I still like to drink. I like the taste of quite a few alcoholic beverages: saké, Irish whiskey, champagne, a good pint of light ale, an ice-cold Pilsner, especially on a hot day.

My immunity to the effects of drink has helped me many times; being able to out-drink everyone in the room can come in handy. I chuckle as I remember out-drinking the Shogun in Dejima in the 1800s, helping my Dutch compatriots earn the right to trade with the locals.

Thinking of the Shogun makes me think of Hiro; they weren't unlike each other. I think of the last time I saw him. Well, not the last time, that was when he climbed into his car and drove off down the hill to the izakaya. No, I think longingly of earlier that morning, when I walked naked into his kitchen to find him, also naked, boiling a kettle to make tea. He turned to smile at me, his penis swinging heavily, still semi-erect after a morning fuck fifteen minutes before. I grinned, touched myself provocatively, then stepped up to him, took his lovely male organ in my hand and kissed him deeply. He turned off the stove, and we repaired to the sitting room floor.

From what I've seen so far, walking along narrow streets to this green, the rebuilding of Orikawa is going well, though there are still very obvious scars from that terrible day. I haven't yet been to the street that Hiro's house was on; I know it was completely destroyed.

The last time I saw Orikawa it was a hellish landscape of rubble: smashed houses, smashed cars, smashed people, a huge carpet of stinking death had been laid lethally over the town. But the Japanese are nothing if not efficient, and especially in Sendai, tenacious in the face of disaster, so for the most part, the rebuilding, the physical rebuilding, is going well. But the mental and emotional rebuilding is slower; ghosts still wander this place. Everybody in the town has some; this town of twenty thousand lost over a thousand people. The online forums have been a good place for people to come together, to mourn, to grieve, to shout and scream, to blame gods and governments, the laws of nature and indeed themselves, often for being lucky that day. 'If only I hadn't gone to [somewhere else] that day, I could have saved [name/s of loved one/s]'.

It starts to rain. I don't have an umbrella, so I take refuge in a little cafe by the green. I sit at a window table and order tea.

As the tea arrives in front of me, I see a familiar face outside, Akio Kurasawa. I wave, he spots me, and with a delighted grin, he comes in to the cafe, and we hug hello. It is, for me, an unexpectedly emotional moment. I've thought about him a lot over the last few years. He has very little to do with the online forums, so I've kind of lost touch with him.

Akio lost his entire family in the tsunami; his mother and father, old and infirm, had a little house right on the coast that was swept away the second the wave made landfall. The remains of his wife's car, identifiable only by its number plate, were found some miles inland, in a ditch by the road, but nothing of her or their son and daughter ever came to light.

And yet he's a remarkably calm man, not exactly cheerful, but cool and collected and not disposed to weeping and wailing when there's work to get on with. A structural engineer who was at a conference in Tokyo at the time of the disaster, he made it back to Orikawa a few days after it happened, hitching lifts in cars and lorries, walking through the night, hoping against hope that some or all of his family had survived. When it turned out that they could not be found, he threw himself into relief work, directing teams clearing rubble, bringing bodies out of smashed houses, loading car carcasses onto low loaders, and, when I first met him, cooking vast pots of rice and soup in the temple. He'd known Hiro too, stopping in the izakaya a couple of times a week for beer and a snack on the way home from work, and he liked him a lot. They would chat about life and love and politics and baseball, "Not necessarily in that order!" as Akio would put it.

And now, here he is, looking a lot older than his thirty-five or so years, but still exuding an air of calm. He sits down opposite me, ordering a green tea latte. "You're here for the memorial unveiling tomorrow?" he asks.

"Yep. Been talking to Haruto Hinata online, he told me about it, so I sort of invited myself. Do you know what form it's going to take?"

"All very simple and low key. Everyone who wants to will gather at the main square at about three thirty. The mayor will say a few words, and the memorial will be unveiled at three forty-five, when the tsunami hit. After that, there's a ceremony up at the temple, and I think some of the bars and restaurants will have things happening too. My friend Akira's nephew, he's a poet, he's going to be doing a reading at Dosia's izakaya in the evening."

"Wow. Emotional stuff, I bet."

"Yes. This town still has a long way to go before its healed itself, generations probably. But doing this sort of thing, honouring the dead, celebrating the living, it helps. Hugely."

Later, we walk arm in arm towards Haruto's place, Akio's umbrella sheltering us from most of the rain, which has become quite heavy. He's checked his weather app; it looks like it should be clear by tomorrow afternoon. At Haruto's he holds my hand and kisses me on the cheek, saying, "Thank you for coming, Shararee. It means a lot to me, to us. To the town." Then he walks on.

Haruto is watching a game show. He puts the kettle on again, we play more Go; I lose heavily. At about nine p.m., he announces he's going to bed. I pop to the 7-Eleven and buy another bottle of saké.

The following day, I rise at nine a.m. and make us tamagoyaki for breakfast. It's a sweet, light, omelette dish, served with a green salad and barbecue sauce. We wash it down with green tea. We play more Go, listening to music on the radio, still saying little. When the news comes on, Haruto turns it down.

At lunchtime, we walk through light drizzle to a cafe, Aikiko's; it's quite a big cafe on the central square near the harbour. In the middle of the square, surrounded by chairs in concentric rows, something about two metres high lurks under a black sheet, tied with a white ribbon — the memorial, I assume. The cafe is very busy, but we squeeze onto two stools at the counter, and, after a couple of griddled scallops to start, we split a large okonomiyaki, ordering Aikiko's celebrated lemony mushroom salad on the side. I have a large Asahi, Haruto sticks with Coke. Aikiko recognises me from five years ago and is touchingly pleased that I've come. She too lost family and friends, like pretty much everyone in Orikawa.

At three twenty or so, I pay our bill; Aikiko closes the cafe. The rain has stopped, the clouds are clearing, and although it is by no means warm, it promises to be a bright, clear day.

Haruto and I take two chairs near the back, and sit silently, watching people arriving, finding seats, sitting with friends and family. The atmosphere is sombre; there are already tears. As she walks up one of the aisles leading to the centre, Sana Hinari, another old acquaintance, spots me and comes over to say hello. I'm delighted to see she's wearing a mayoral chain, and she's clearly impressed that I've chosen to be here today; we worked long, hard hours alongside one another five years ago. She gives me a warm hug, shakes hands with Haruto, then goes to the memorial, where she's handed a microphone. The audience settles, quietens.

"Five years ago, today," she says when all is silent, her amplified voice echoing across the square, "Death came to Orikawa. The tsunami that struck us that day was the biggest modern Japan has ever witnessed. Orikawa lost one thousand and ninety-two people, missing or dead. Everyone in this town lost friends and family. It was a terrible time, one that I hope we never have to live through again.

"And yet, this is still Orikawa. This is still our town, this is still our home, and in the five years since, we have done a great job of rebuilding it. The rubble, the smashed up houses, the crushed cars and boats, they've all been cleared away, and with the help of grants from central government, we have rebuilt a lot of buildings and roads and indeed the new promenade was opened just over a year after the old one was swept away. There is still more work to do, but I know Orikawa will do it. For the sake of our departed loved ones, wherever they may be, and our beloved citizens, Orikawa will do it; Orikawa must do it. This memorial, paid for by donations by townspeople, has all the names of the missing and dead on it. We shall honour them." And she tugs on the white ribbon, and the black sheet falls to the ground, revealing a black marble monolith, tall, rectangular, with white kanji inscribed on it. "Please, you may come up and inspect it."

Haruto and I sit for a while till the crowd around the memorial has thinned considerably, then we walk up to it, hand in hand. I find Hiro's name almost immediately, and, tracing the kanji with my fingers, I can't help the tears. The huge sense of loss, not only for me, and for Orikawa, but for the Immortals as a community, is almost overwhelming; I want to howl my grief to the sky, I want to scream it up into the…

Then there's a loud, drawn-out moan from beside me and I turn, expecting to see Haruto in a similar emotional state. But it's me he's staring at, not the memorial. His hand comes up, a shaking finger pointing at me, tears streaming from his eyes, a look of horror on his suddenly pale face. And, for a brief, fleeting, almost non-existent moment, I Sense him.

"What — what — what?" he gasps. "What are you?" And then he turns, and stumbles away, bumping people aside, knocking over chairs, heading towards the harbour.

I find Haruto on a bench on the new promenade. Nobody made too much of a fuss as I stared open mouthed after him, but when I set off to follow him, there was a rising buzz of conversation behind me, part of which was the word gaijin. As I walk up to him, not Sensing him now, he looks up, startled. "No, don't. I don't... I can't," he says. "Please, just go. My front door is unlocked. Get your bag and leave my—"

"No!" I snap. "Not until you tell me... not until... Look... are you... are you Very Very Old?"

Confusion appears on his face. "Very... what? What do you mean?"

"What age are you?" I hiss. "When were you born?"

"What? What are you talking about?"

"Just tell me. Please. Then I'll leave you in peace."

"I'm sixty-one. I'll be sixty-two next month. I was born in 1955. I have told you this before, in our online messages. Why?"

"I'm... well... what age do you think I am?"

"I don't know, fifty-eight, fifty-nine, maybe sixty?"

"I'm... put it this way. I'm the same age as Hiro was."

"About sixty-five?"

"No... I... look... let's wind back a bit. What was all that 'what are you' stuff about up at the memorial?"

Unexpectedly, tears come to Haruto's eyes, and he looks down at his feet. "I need a drink," he says. "At home. Let's go to my house."

We don't talk as we walk to his house. On the way, I buy saké and beer.

When we reach his kitchen, Haruto reaches up to a top shelf, and takes down a packet of Mevius cigarettes and a lighter. He places an Asahi ashtray on the table in the sitting room. Then he gets out two little saké glasses, and two big beer glasses. We sit and pour each other shots of saké, as custom dictates in Japan. We say 'kanpai', clicking our glasses together, and drink. We set our glasses down. We light cigarettes.

"I want to talk about Hiro," Haruto says.

"OK," I say.

"And about you," he says.

"OK," I say, a little more warily. I'm still thrown by the fact that I 'Sensed' someone who appears to be a mortal, though the fact that I can't now is confusing me even more.

"I met Hiro soon after I moved to Orikawa, 1994 it was. I was thirty-eight," he says. "I worked for NNK, Nihon No Kaiyokogaku, it's a marine engineering company, and they wanted me to head the new regional office in Ishinomaki. I met him in the izakaya a week or so after I arrived. We got on very well, we became friends quickly. Saw each other most days, ate together, drank together, watched films together, played Go together, argued about sports; he was a Giants fan, I follow the Tigers. He was a happy man, funny, relaxed, contented—" He pauses, and opens a can of beer, pours some into a glass, and hands it to me. I do the same for him. "But... occasionally, when I was with him," he says, "I kind of... felt something I didn't... understand."

"What was that?"

"I felt... it was physical. It was a kind of... itch. No, that's not right. More of a tickle. But inside my head, you know?" He taps his temple. "Just about here." He's describing the Sense, as far as I'm concerned. Different Sensers feel it in different ways, but this is more or less how I feel it.

"How often did it happen?"

"Once in, what is the English expression? Once in a blue moon. Maybe a dozen times in the seventeen years I knew him. Sometimes it was fleeting, sometimes it would stay for a few minutes. Once, I was sitting here reading the newspaper in the evening, and I suddenly knew he was walking up the road, and was about to knock on my door. And he did, a minute later." He lights a cigarette from the butt of the last one, and stubs the latter out in the ashtray. "Do you know what I mean?" he asks, looking me in the eye.

I hesitate. Then I say, "Yes. I do."

"I felt it from you, briefly, at the memorial. That's why I ran away."

"I know. I felt it too," I say, wondering if the emotional intensity of the moment brought it on.

"What is it?" he asks.

"I… I can't tell you. It's nothing bad, nothing dangerous or scary. But I can't tell you."

"Can't?" he says. "Or won't?"

"Both," I say.

I expect him to press it, but instead he says, "OK. What about you? How did you meet him?"

I've been kind of waiting for this question, and I have a fairly good idea of the back-story Hiro had created for himself, and where I slot into it. "We met a long time ago," I say. This is no less than the truth; we actually knew each other, on and off, nearly four hundred years, meeting in the court of Sigismund the Third, King of Poland. But Haruto doesn't need to know that. "In Los Angeles, where I live. He came to the US in the '60s to study aeronautics. But he didn't much like LA, so he came back to Japan in the late '70s."

"And you came to visit him here a couple of times."

"Yes, in '82 and '93 and, of course, 2011. We kept in touch by letter and email. He visited me too, in eighty-eight and 2002."

Haruto nods, and throws his saké back. I fill his glass again. "I went to Kyoto last year," he says. "Where Hiro said he came from originally. Where he said his family had an izakaya. I could find no izakaya run by a Watanabe family."

"No?" I said, cautiously. "Maybe it's closed down."

He shook his head. "I spoke to my cousin there, he had a friend who worked for the city, in charge of restaurant and bar licencing. He could find no Watanabe izakaya either."

I shrug. "Maybe Hiro massaged the truth, maybe his family didn't own one, they just worked in someone else's."

"Maybe. But then he never mentioned his family that much either. Did he talk about them with you?"

"No, not really. His parents died before I met him. And he had no siblings."

Haruto grunts. Then he pours the last of the saké into our glasses. I realise he's approaching drunk, his eyes defocused, his lips wet, and he's chain smoking.

"Can I ask you a question?" I say.

"Of course."

"Did you ever talk to Hiro about this... feeling?"

"No."

"Why not?"

He drags deep from his cigarette, then swigs beer, some splashing on his shirt.

"I... I didn't want to... I thought he'd find it... creepy. I thought maybe it would affect our friendship. I'm not... I've never been the sort of person who makes friends easily. He was my best friend, and I didn't want him to think I was weird. And I've spoken to no one else about it either. Other than you."

He gets up unsteadily from the table and, beer glass in hand, slumps on the sofa. "Hiro, Hiro, Hiro," he says, with such sadness in his voice and eyes I suddenly tear up. "You were such a good man." He lifts his beer glass in a toast, then drains it and puts it on the floor, where it falls over and rolls under the sofa. "I loved you," he says very softly. His head nods forward and his eyes close. Minutes later, he's snoring. I open another beer.

Haruto wakes a couple of hours later. I've eased him into a more comfortable position on the sofa, and put a blanket over him. He is, of course, dreadfully embarrassed by his falling asleep, but I assure him it's of no import.

I make poached eggs on toast, and we eat them in silence. We drink green tea, and we watch some of the TV coverage of this fifth anniversary of the tsunami. At about nine o'clock, Haruto turns off the TV.

"You are going back to Tokyo tomorrow?" he asks.

"Yes, and then back to America," I lie.

"We won't see each other again." It's a statement of fact, not a question.

"Oh, I don't know, maybe in a couple of years..." Another lie.

"No."

"Why not?"

"You know Osaka is the centre of cancer research in Japan, yes?"

"No, I didn't know that."

"That's where I was on the day of the tsunami, remember."

"Ah. Yes." I realise he's never told me why he was in Osaka, this day five years ago.

"Yes. The treatment worked for a couple of years, but a few months ago…" He pinches the bridge of his nose and closes his eyes.

"How long?" I ask.

"Maybe six months. Probably less."

"Do many people know?"

"No, only my doctor and lawyer. The oncologists in Osaka. I never told Hiro."

"I'm so sorry to hear that, Haruto." I take his hands in mine.

He smiles ruefully. "Maybe I'll be meeting Hiro soon, maybe I'll find out what happened to him that day."

"I'm sure he'll be delighted to see you again, please give him my love," I say.

He goes to bed a few minutes later. I go back to the bench on the green with more saké and cigarettes, and I cry and I cry and I cry.

Later, in bed, I come to a very easy decision. I will definitely not be telling any Immortals about what has happened between Haruto and me today, especially any involved with VVO. The nightmare scenario of some over-curious VVO operative turning up on Haruto's doorstep with a knife in his hand, eager to find out if he really is a mere mortal, is too horrifying to contemplate.

The following morning, Haruto drives me to the bus station. Both of us moist-eyed, we hug briefly, I kiss his cheek, then I climb aboard the bus.

A few hours later, I'm back at Ginza Conrad Six. A quick visit to the Daimaru food court in the basement, and I'm ready.

I empty carrier bags onto the table in the kitchen, put some of the contents in the fridge, then eat my way steadily through the rest; microwaved mac and cheese ready meals mostly, but also rice, fish balls, salads, deep fried chicken nuggets, and a family sized packet of mashed potato. I have to wash the last of it down with milky tea, nearly gagging as I do, feeling horribly full and corpulent. Then I lock the earthquake-proof metal front door and walk around the apartment making sure everything is ready, drawing the curtains throughout.

I strip off, and stand naked in front of the full-length mirror. I see what looks like a woman in her seventies, a woman who appears to be in the twilight of her life. While the hair is a fashionable bob, it is entirely white, below it a narrow, lined face, rheumy grey eyes, and a turkey-wattled neck above small, droopy breasts, a saggy pot belly and skinny white legs. Of course I know that this is just appearance; I'm as fit as a flea, a few months ago I easily fought off two muggers who tried to relieve me of my handbag while I was walking in LA.

But it's time for a change; this aged suit of flesh has got to go. I clean my teeth, trim my nails and shave my head.

In the bedroom, I check the house's security system from the terminal by the bed and tap the key that puts the whole place in lockdown.

Everything is quiet and secure.

So I start to hum my little tune, the one I use to lead me into the chants that lead me into the mental exercises that lead me into the Sleep. It makes me feel Sleepy, it makes me feel old, it makes me feel scared, it makes me feel exhilarated. My legs weaken, my breathing becomes shallow and laboured. Still humming, I lie down on the bed.

I think of locking the front door as the last act of Shirley Mitford. My new identity, back referenced by VVO into several hacked databases around the world, will be Maxine Glass. Allegedly born in England in 1994, both my parents are dead and I am of 'independent means'. I have no siblings or other living relatives. Shirley Mitford, who will 'disappear', has already passed on ownership of several holding companies to companies owned by Maxine Glass.

Seamlessly, I move from hum to chant, a series of coherent, meaningless semi-sung 'words' I can't reproduce without the prior humming, yet which now come as naturally as breathing. I have no idea what the words mean, even what language they're in, but almost immediately, my body starts to feel heavy and soft. Already, as I sink into the bed, I can see/feel the images and text start to coalesce and tetris together out of the corner of my mind's eye. My body feels heavier and heavier and my eyelids slide closed, squeezing out tears that trickle past my ears and onto the pillow. Sometimes, a mental piece goes astray, and I have to move it about in my imagination, into the right position, sometimes an equation... drifts into sight and I have to... to solve it, sometimes... a shape... it... morphs and a number... fumbles and an idea... smiles and the light... flows with warmth... and there... are colours and... and... and...

We Immortals have been filthy rich and pretty powerful for as long as any of us can remember, so finding somewhere to Sleep has never been a problem, indeed in the last hundred years or so, The Long Labs, particularly LL Four, have been looking for volunteers to be closely observed - x-rays, MRI, CAT scans — as they Sleep, and have been providing a safe place to do so. In my case, almost all of my Sleeps have been in buildings I've owned and had adapted to my own needs. Upon waking, it used to be easy enough to move on out into the world, setting up a new identity as we went. Ever since the advent of electrics, then electronics, then the digital age, it has become much more difficult; everyone has to have not just a cardboard book with their photo stuck to it, but a record of that cardboard book on a computer disk somewhere; lately that cardboard book has had to have an RFID (radio frequency identification) chip embedded in it too. Luckily, there are a few Immortals who were in at the ground floor when it came to the Internet, and they've been instrumental in helping the rest of us set up new IDs; indeed, it's become a standard service at VVO. It also helps that, in the UK, where my new ID is registered, I have a Very Very Old friend at the Passport Office.

And... and... and the noise of my stomach growling wakes me up. Or maybe it's the urgent need for a piss. Or the thick layer of itchy grey fluff all over me.

For a minute or two, I blink and breathe and wriggle and squirm and stretch, then I sit up and tap the mouse and the display wakes up and tells me it's mid-morning, twenty-seven days later. I sit on the toilet, and have a long, long, dark brown piss, clumps of fluff falling off me onto the bathroom floor. I haven't seen myself in the mirror yet.

Then I'm in the shower, loving how good my body feels and looks under my hands, the legs and arms smooth and strong, the stomach flat and hard, the breasts full and firm, no longer drooping and swingy. Then I'm out of the shower, and I'm towelling myself off, my skin feeling young and taut. Then I look in the full-length mirror.

This moment always takes my breath away, despite my having done it many times. I have great hair; snow white a few weeks ago, it's now a couple of inches long and jet black. The scar on my neck, the result of a car accident in LA a few years ago, is gone. My eyes look clear and healthy, and have changed from grey to hazel. In effect, I've unaged by several decades, and now can pass for twenty-five or younger. Even my teeth look good, though my finger and toenails need to be trimmed.

Manicured, pedicured, dried and dressed, I put the kettle on, and put a fish pie and a macaroni cheese into the microwave. At this post Sleep stage, I am always ravenously hungry, and need a good couple of thousand calories, despite the vast meal taken shortly before my extended nap. My food ready, I sit down and begin to eat, washing it down with sweet, milky coffee. I look at some news sites to catch up with what's going on in the world; floods have killed hundreds in Bangladesh, there's been a truck attack in France, a mass shooting in America, and another in Peru. I check in on www.veryveryold.com. There are no new messages for me, and nothing hugely interesting in the timeline; I update my profile to include my new name.

I don't leave the apartment today, instead pottering about slowly, grazing in the kitchen, trying not to think about alcohol, with a TV on in every room, mostly tuned to the BBC so I can practise my new English accent. In the evening, I have a coded phone conversation with that Very Very Old friend in the UK Passport Office, sending him a head and shoulders selfie taken against my white kitchen wall. I make sure Maxine Glass's bank accounts and credit cards are all OK; they were set up a good year ago, and I've been monitoring them ever since. I resist the temptation to open a bottle of saké or a six-pack of Asahi, instead sticking with tea and coffee, and by ten p.m., I'm in bed and lying down with the iPad, still catching up. The following day, I start my new life.

Geoffrey Mitchell in Rome

I'm an atheist. I always have been, even when I was pope.

Mind you, if you wanted to be Holy Father, Bishop of Rome and ex officio leader of the worldwide Catholic Church in the 1500s, you didn't need to believe in God, you just needed to be rich, well connected and well versed in the uses of murder, torture and all the other unpleasantries the Firm ran on in those days. Oh, and having a knowledge of ritual and liturgy helped too, though you had minions to remember that for you.

Soon after sunrise, I lock the front door, and walk uphill, then downhill, to the Vatican. I eat a light breakfast in a tiny cafe, then I take a tour, for old times' sake: the museums, Raphael's Rooms, the Sistine Chapel, St Peter's Square and of course the basilica. I have to stifle laughs every now and then, listening to my fellow tourists going on about the holiness and serenity of the basilica. I toy with the idea of telling them how it wasn't always thus, as I'm sure the serving girl I had a fuck with there would attest if she hadn't died nearly five hundred years ago, but I keep it to myself. I stand under Sebastiano del Piombo's portrait of me, and wink and smile at the goth in the Cradle of Filth teeshirt, but he doesn't seem to notice the likeness, giving me instead a baleful, eyelinered stare.

There is, however, only so much holy art one can take in one go, especially when one actually lived amid it for over a decade. On any other day, I'd go and giggle at some Caravaggios, but today I've got stuff to do, so I head back to Trastevere. By midday, I'm ensconced in a window seat at Giselda with a small, strong espresso, a large, blue Sambuca and a tall glass of ice-cold sparkling water. As I sip, I think about what I'm about to do, and why I'm about to do it.

Just over a year ago, I had a visit from the Very Very Old organisation. I was in Istanbul for the publication of my then new novel, staying alone in a huge riverfront mansion that I had borrowed from a real live (Immortal) Ottoman prince. The morning before the publication date, I was out on the riverside terrace answering emails, when my iPhone vibrated on the table. It was a number I didn't recognise, so I didn't answer. A moment later, a text from the same number — three letters, all capitals, a sharp consonant twice, and a fat vowel once. I sighed, and called the number.

"So, you're VVO," I said as we took a table at O Balik Yeri, a great fish restaurant a short walk away from the house, one I'd been in every day that week. The 'Please stop dropping public hints about being Immortal' conversation with VVO was always more relaxed over a decent lunch, and I couldn't be arsed cooking.

"Yes," said Zeynep Aksoy. Seeming thirty or so, she wore a well-cut grey Balenciaga suit. I was in trackies, trainers and a manky old Motörhead teeshirt. I'd ordered the same meal for both of us as we arrived, a kind of bouillabaisse reduction to start, followed by their legendary fish-in-a-bag — fillets of that day's catch baked in paper bags with all sorts of fantastic liquors and vegetables and herbs and whatever else the chef felt would be good. The place smelt divine; my stomach growled, then Zeynep's did, and we laughed together. A carafe of house white was put in front of us, and two glasses. I poured, and we drank.

"And you are, I take it, here on official VVO business."

"Well, yes and no. I suppose I should start by saying that I really like your books."

"You're not just saying that to soften me up?"

"No, not at all. They're exciting and involving and interesting, and I love the texture and depth you give them, they come across as very authentic."

"And you should know."

"Yep, there was even one of them, San Juan Bautista, I was involved with, in a small way."

"Oh yeah? How so? Oh, thank you," I said as the waiter put down our starters. I took up a teaspoon, and tasted the soup. Served at room temperature in little coffee cups, it was rich and velvety smooth, with a fantastically intense fishy, prawny flavour — just a hint of pastis and fennel in the background. Zeynep seemed to like it too.

"I was on one of the other ships, the *Secilia,*" she said, "We went down on the coast of County Clare soon after the *Bautista* did. Ended up living there for a few years. Lovely place."

"And yet you're here to tell me to stop it."

"No. Well, yes. Not to stop writing the books. VVO has no problem with you writing historical novels. But there are concerns about the constant flow of, you know, your historical details. The ones no one else seems to know about. The ones that Simon Schama wrote about as being — and I quote — 'very very believable indeed, almost as if Mr Mitchell had been there'."

"Or, as he later said in the same review — and I quote — *'Mr Mitchell is of course very imaginative, and it's this imagination, this extrapolation of what is known about whatever century or country his stories are set in, that makes us historians simultaneously delighted and enraged when we read his novels'.* Saturday Guardian, Review section, June 2003."

"And it makes VVO nervous, you know that," she said. "You've even been proven right, so to speak, on a couple of occasions."

"Leading VVO to think people will jump to the inescapable conclusion that the reason I've mentioned, say, match swinging on the deck of a Spanish warship ten years before anyone else is that I was actually there, five hundred odd years ago, and not because I'm making perfectly reasonable things up, and sometimes guessing right. And that will lead them to the further conclusion that I'm not unique, that there's some sort of, I don't know, secret cabal, you know, like the Illuminati or the Bilderberg group, only older and scarier."

"In a nutshell, yes."

I scraped up the last few drops of the soup, then set my spoon down in the saucer. "Hang on, we're not the Illuminati, are we?" I asked.

"No, as far as I know, we're not." She laughed. "Although we surely must have at least one representative in the Bilderberg group."

"It'd be foolish not to."

"So, your latest book…"

"*Rings Faint the Spanish Gun*, it's called, set here. In the bookshops tomorrow, as well you know."

"And it has all the usual touches? The immersively described setting, the blend of fact and fiction, the little details that make it seem so real?"

"Yep."

"Like what?"

"I can recommend a bookshop not far from here, you can buy your own copy, though there may be a queue. Pop back and I'll sign it if you like, in any of a couple of dozen languages. Ah, look, here comes our fish. Come on, let's forget the main reason you're here, and do justice to Hamid's cooking."

Later, we strolled in Yildiz Park. Lunch had, of course, been wonderful, and I discreetly burped sweet fishy burps as we came to the top of the hill and sat on a bench by the pond.

"You know you're on a hiding to nothing," I said, lighting two cigarettes and passing her one.

"Yes. But I was tasked with passing on VVO's concerns, and for the record, pass them on I will. The message is, in simple terms, be careful, you're pissing a lot of people off."

"And if I choose to ignore such an elegantly delivered warning, what are you going to do, kill me?"

"No, that'd be silly. VVO don't want any more attention drawn to you than you have yourself. But they do have friends in high places, including those with controlling interests in publishing companies."

"So you're going to lean on Penguin until they suddenly tell one of their biggest selling authors to fuck off?"

"Why not? VVO are powerful, and wealthy."

She did, I had to admit, have a point. Being two thousand or more years old gave one lots of chances to become fabulously rich, and VVO were astute investors, and they could play a very long game.

"OK, I suppose that constitutes a sort of threat," I conceded.

"Sort of."

I sighed. "Look, to be honest, you may have come at the right time anyway. I'm starting to run out of steam with the novels. No, that's not true, not so much run out of steam, it's just that I'm getting a hankering to move on and... I don't know... maybe do something else."

I didn't add some recent musings on where this life was going; I was indeed starting to think of moving on, maybe Sleep in the next year, probably in my house in New York, then head for Canada, then do some sort of road trip through the States and Mexico down to, well, whatever country it is at the bottom of the Americas, take a couple of decades to do it.

"Will you continue writing novels?"

"I don't know. I have two more books planned over the next couple of years.

"And will they have all the usual touches?"

"You'll have to wait and see."

Eight months ago, on a night off from finishing my book, *Lowonida*, I was in a pub in West London, and I was overheard telling a story to some mortals about the Emperor Constantine the Great by a VVO agent called Joseph Green. I'd met him before, the short-arsed little wanker, he had no sense of humour, and I was pretty sure his presence that night was no coincidence; he was, after all, a Senser. I saw him standing nearby as I was wrapping up my story, so I got up, walked past him and ordered a pint at the bar. As soon as I had my beer, I nipped out for a cigarette, knowing he'd follow me, indeed I held the door open for him.

"I mean," he said, once we'd both lit up, "It's bad enough that you've put yourself in the public eye with those trashy historical novels you insist on publishing, but ending a long, drawn out, unfunny story about events in the third century with 'And I should know, because I was there' is just asking for trouble. I mean, you were a VVO agent for nearly a century, you know the drill."

"It got a laugh," I said, "although it might have been a bit too meta for you."

"Meta?"

"You know I've been a novelist for a lot longer than I was ever a VVO agent."

"I'm well aware of—"

"And one of the things my readers love is the historical detail."

"If you say so, I don't care. I just—"

"Which is why that throwaway line got a laugh. And anyway, do you honestly think anyone listening had the remotest suspicion I was telling the truth? Do you really think they believed me? Come on."

"But that's not—"

"Also, by the way, trashy? Fuck off."

"Mr Mitchell. VVO don't do anything to attract non-Immortals' attention to our longevity. Anything. Even in jest."

"As well you know, I walked out of VVO after the Husayn Pasha debacle, so I couldn't give a fuck what they think. Also, it doesn't matter that the books are semi-autobiographical, it's still great storytelling, and I take a huge amount of pride in the thirty-four novels I've published as Geoffrey Mitchell, not to mention the hundreds of other stories I've written over the centuries." I drew deep on my cigarette, then dropped it into the gutter. "How many of them have you actually read?"

"I've never read any of them. But I'm told they sell well in airports and bus stations." He smirked.

"You're a prick, you know that?" I said, and picked up my pint and went back into the bar. He followed me.

And that's the guts of the conversation I had that evening with Joseph Green.

I moved on to another pub; he tried to tag along, but in the next place a rock band was playing, good noisy thrashy stuff. It meant we couldn't talk without shouting into each other's ear, so he sloped off half an hour later.

I'd never got on well with VVO over the centuries, they are conservative, interfering and self-serving. As bad as the Catholic Church in many ways. So I was happy not to come into contact with them too often, and what with there only being a few hundred agents at any given time, I mostly did OK, even with my upper-middle rank celebrity status in the mortal world. Mostly.

It's nearing the time agreed, so I pay my bill and walk out onto Via di San Francesco a Ripa. It's a nice May day, bright and warm, and I sling my jacket over my shoulder, and walk towards the apartment in shirt sleeves.

A month ago, *Lowonida,* the novel I planned to be my second last, was finally published. It very nearly wasn't. There was trouble with the very first print run; somehow the version that the editors signed off on wasn't the version that ended up at the printers. Instead the one they got was a couple of months old, with all the continuity errors and grammar mistakes I thought I'd ironed out. Fortunately, they'd only printed off a couple of hundred review copies when someone noticed, thankfully before they were sent out. Those copies got pulped, and the publishers and I made damn sure the version that then went to the printers was the finished article. I had an online security specialist do a full diagnostic on my setup, wondering how the earlier version had escaped my archive, but they found nothing untoward. Paranoid, I didn't call on any of the usual internet savvy Immortals to assist; I couldn't help but wonder if some VVO whizz kid had hacked into my systems, and/or those of the publishers or printers, and fucked with those files.

Then the correct review copies went out, and almost immediately, the book got some appalling write-ups. A BBC reviewer, a mortal I had previously had a good relationship with, tore it to pieces, and when my agent tried to contact him, by phone, text and email, he was unavailable. The same happened with a reviewer at the New York Times, one who'd previously loved my work.

Then the book was published, and sales were, well, muted. Normally, if they didn't come out at the same time as a Jack Reacher, my novels were in the top five within a week. This time it took three weeks to dent the top twenty. There were distribution problems too, and formatting errors on Kindles and iPads; it got a lot of one-star reviews on Amazon for that reason alone. My agent, not an Immortal, told me there was nothing to worry about, that it was just a blip in an otherwise stratospheric trajectory, but I wasn't so sure. Then last week, in my London penthouse, I watched the book getting pulled to bits on some late-night literary TV wankfest. Grumpy and pissed off, and fuelled by a bottle of tequila, a lump of hashish and a gram of very decent cocaine, I had an idea, a fucking big idea. Almost a fucking epiphany, it was. And that's how I ended up ringing my agent at three a.m., and making him an offer he couldn't refuse.

She's early, standing outside the block when I arrive. She has a copy of the magazine she writes for in her hand. She's very tall, slim to the point of emaciation, seems about forty, and is wearing a tight, black jumpsuit. Her long, ash blonde hair is tied into a pony tail. Behind her, a short, dark man, festooned with camera equipment, is fiddling with an iPhone.

"Good morning, Mr Mitchell," she says in Italian. "Nice to meet you. I'm Chiara Congliani. This is Paulo

Metti, he'll take a few photos before we start, then it'll just be us."

"Good morning," I say, extending a hand. She shakes limply; his grip is like a vice.

I let us into the rented apartment. A rooftop place, it's light and bright and airy, with a decent-sized terrace with tables and umbrellas, a well-stocked bar and the sort of basics — tomatoes, mozzarella, fresh herbs, pasta, olive oil — that any half-decent Roman kitchen should have in it. Last night, when I first saw it, I walked around the place, mapping it in my head, deciding where to hold the interview. This morning, I put some cushions on the timber benches on the L-shaped terrace, made sure there was white wine, Aperol, Prosecco and San Pellegrino in the fridge and went to look at the Holy City.

She seems to like the apartment. She walks from room to room, making comments in a faintly Neapolitan accent. She loves the view of the Orto Botanico from the terrace. She accepts a glass of white wine, spritzed with sparkling water. Her photographer takes some snaps while we walk about, then, after a few more formally posed pictures out on the terrace, he leaves us to it. She takes a little voice recorder out, and sets it down on the low table between us. I see a copy of *Lowonida* poking out of her bag. She starts the recorder, and opens a notebook. "OK, I'll start with a couple of standard questions," she says.

"OK."

"What is your full name?" she asks.

"My name is Geoffrey Alan Mitchell."

"And what is your age?"

"It says I'm seventy-three on my passport."

"Where do you call home?"

"I have homes in New York, Pondicherry and Tokyo."

"Not Rome?"

"Not at the moment. This place is rented."

"Is there love in your life?"

"Love? What, as in a partner, a wife?"

"Or a lover or a husband?"

"There was a Mrs Mitchell in the nineties, but we parted." I don't add that it was in the 1890s.

"OK. So." She pauses and sips. "I'd like to start the interview proper with what the public know best about you, your novels. You've published thirty-four of them, starting in 1981, and they've all been best sellers."

"With the possible exception of this one," I say, nodding at her copy of *Lowonida*.

"Really? I had a look at the sales figures before I left the office, and it's doing pretty well. Ten thousand copies in the first month. I'd say that's a decent figure."

"Normally I sell ten thousand in the first week. I've been known to sell four or five thousand on the first day. Especially Kindle editions."

"So what happened with *Lowonida*? It is, I have to say, an excellent book."

"Thank you. I think, to be honest, that there are people who have an interest in it selling badly."

"You do?" she says, frowning. "Who are they?"

I take a deep breath. Then I say, "An organisation called Very Very Old, known as VVO."

"And what does it do, this Very Very Old?"

"It looks after the interests of living people who are some two thousand years old."

"Um, what? People who are…" She looks utterly confused.

"Two thousand years old. Or older."

"Is this… I mean… two thousand years old? That's impossible."

"No, no it isn't. I am one of them. My earliest memory is of a battle between the Sarmatians and the Scythians. Around 10 or 20 AD as far as I can tell. I survived having my throat cut that day."

"You're two thousand years old. You're some sort of indestructible superman."

"Kind of. In fact, my memory goes back two thousand years or so, but I don't remember a childhood, so I could actually be much older. And while I'm no superman, I do heal very quickly; I've got over wounds and bodily traumas that would kill non-Immortals."

"But I don't… Oh, hang on," she smiles, nods, makes a note. "This is some kind of… is this you trying out a new, I don't know, a new plot? Are you moving into Sci-fi?"

"No, I really, really am at least two thousand years old. This is not some sort of plot device trial run."

"No, you're not, no one is. Come on. You're a novelist, an imaginative novelist. You're better than this."

"But… OK, let me try to convince you another way."

And I get up from my seat, and go into the kitchen and return with a large, wickedly sharp, chopping knife from the wall-mounted, magnetic knife block, and a roll of kitchen paper. I sit back down, put my left hand flat on the table, palm down, and before she can stop me, I raise the knife in my right hand, and bring it down sharply, the razor sharp tip penetrating the back of my left hand, sliding between the tendons and bones there, and into the wooden surface of the table between us. A part of my mind notes that I won't get all of my deposit back from the owners of the apartment. As she jumps to her feet, her hand going to her mouth, her chair falling over backwards, I take my right hand away and sit there, the knife upright, trembling slightly, pinning me to the table, blood starting to seep from the wound. It is incredibly painful.

"What the fuck are you doing?" she gasps. I pull the knife out and put it flat on the table, my blood on the tip of the blade. I hold my left hand up so she can see the wound, and I turn it back and forth so she can see the knife has gone right through. Then I pick up the kitchen roll, and wind it about my hand, pressing it against the wound.

"It'll stop hurting in about ten minutes. In about forty-five minutes, I'll unwrap it and you will see that it has healed. Will that convince you that there's something in what I've been saying?"

"No, it'll convince me that you're fucking mentally ill. I'm leaving, right now." She snatches up her bag, stuffing her recorder and notebook into it.

"And leaving quite a story?"

"What, Famous Writer Turns Out To Be Self Harming Nutjob? No, not the sort of story I want to be known for. Whatever fantasy you're trying to involve me in, whatever sort of, I don't know, unpleasant publicity stunt this is, I'm not being a party to it." And she turns and walks back into the apartment. Moments later, I hear the front door slam.

She's back twenty-five minutes later. In the meantime, I've righted her chair, had a cigarette and a glass of wine, and I've jotted down some notes for Geoffrey Mitchell's last novel, *The Man From Thuringia*. It has also occurred to me to dedicate it to VVO and/or Chiara Congliani when I publish it. The wound in my hand has stopped hurting. I let her in without a word, and we take our positions again on the terrace.

"Why did you come back?" I ask.

She laughs. She has clearly calmed down. "Come on, it'd be foolish not to. Whatever scam, stunt, plot you're running, my curiosity has the better of me. You're a clever writer, and you obviously have something interesting going on."

"Have you told anyone about this?"

"No. I went to a cafe by the river and had a quiet word with myself over a caffe corretto."

"Good, I'm glad. You won't be disappointed."

"We'll see about that," she says, taking her notebook and recorder out again. "Shall we start?"

This time, I go first with some questions.

"So how many of my novels have you read?"

"All of them."

"In order?"

"No. My first one was *Houndsditch*, I read that a few months after it came out. And then I went back to *The First Story*, and worked my way forward. Now I always buy them as soon as they come out."

"Excellent. So, what's your favourite?"

"My favourite?" she pauses, sips wine. "Difficult. Might be *Ichneumon*, the one with Charles Darwin in it. That's superb. But... no, I think the one I enjoy the most is *The Other Orlando*."

"Interesting choice. Untypical it is, not quite as straightforward as most of the others. Quite experimental for me."

"The multiple timeline approach is unique among your books, as is the open-ended denouement. But it is just so enjoyable, so... so immersive. The first time I read it I did so in one sitting, finished it at the kitchen table at two a.m., my eyes were stinging, my back was aching, and I realised I'd been bursting for a pee for an hour. Your central character, Nathaniel, he was very believable, very... well, I mean, he was an asshole for most of the book, but his motivation for everything he did, good or bad, was very well justified, beautifully written."

"Thank you. You know Nathaniel was me?"

"I have wondered," She laughed. "I mean, the main characters in your books tend to be quite similar; resourceful and brave, sarcastic and unfriendly, often quite mercenary and dishonest. But they do tend to have a caring, gentle side that occasionally leads to their downfall, albeit temporarily; they stand up for the little guy. They also learn and change, they have a fascinating adventure with a real figure from history as a sidekick, they defeat the bad guys, get the girl, or the boy, and move on, much happier and more contented than they were at the beginning. They've often helped solve some local, social wrong too."

"You have been paying attention, haven't you?" I take out my cigarettes, and offer her one. She declines. I light up.

"You always narrate in the first-person present tense; in twenty-one of the thirty-four novels you've published, the main character is male, and apart from the ungendered, unnamed protagonist in *Deijima; An Object Lesson in Bribery and Corruption*, all the rest are female. Also, you write a damn good sex scene, though you're clearly not heterosexual."

"Thank you. Either you've got a very good research department, or you truly are a fan."

"I truly am a fan."

"Good. So. Where do you think I get my ideas?" I finish the dregs of my wine, and pour another, and one for her too.

"Well, where does any novelist get their ideas? Life, surroundings, incidents, their imagination."

"Which is how I work too. It's just that… well, a lot of the stories I've written have come from things that have really happened to me. *The Lady and Her Restoration*, for instance, you remember that?"

"Yes, I loved it. And so did my mother, I bought it for her."

"Well, tell her this; I really was in London in 1660. I really did deliver a copy of *The Declaration of Breda* to The Lord Mayor, paid to do so by Charles the Second. OK, so I didn't get caught up in a web of intrigue and fear resulting in a mad dash on horseback across the countryside to Norfolk in the middle of the night, that did indeed come from my imagination, but the bones of that book lay in those few days I spent in London that year. And *The Lady Straven* was based on a young lady I spent some of those days with, although she was no lady."

"Right," she stretches the word out, left eyebrow arching. "Three hundred and fifty years ago."

"Three hundred and fifty-six."

"This is where it all falls to the ground for me. I find this very disappointing."

"Disappointing?"

"Why are you doing this, why don't you just say 'Look at me, I can write great stories'? This is demeaning. Why are you claiming the clearly impossible?"

"Who says it's impossible?"

"Me! Science! People don't live two thousand years! I'm pretty sure we would have heard if it were true."

"Maybe you are, right now. Bear in mind, when I take this off," I hold up my left hand, still wrapped in kitchen paper, "you'll have to do a big rethink."

"Yeah, right," she says, and sighs. "Look, I saw Penn & Teller do something like that a few years ago. Utterly believable it was, until they showed you how it was done. It was only when I was having my coffee round the corner that I remembered it. The fake knife, the blood capsule. You could easily—"

"The knife mark in the table?" I say, pointing. I've cleaned up the blood and put the knife away, but the slim, triangular hole is very much in evidence.

"You could have done that before I even got here."

"OK, you do it then. I'll put my hand on the table and you stick the knife through it. It'll be fucking painful, but it'd convince you I'm not faking it."

"Mr Mitchell, please. You absolutely know I'm going to refuse to stab you. Let's just pretend you didn't even say that. OK?" There's a crease of anger between her eyes.

"Whatever."

"So, when you show me your undamaged hand, as I'm assuming you will soon, what earthly difference will that make? You could have faked it. What then?"

"We could go through some of my stories, and I could give you the real-life version of each one. I could tell you how, when I was pope in the 1520s—"

"The pope? You were the pope? What the—"

"Pope Clement the Seventh."

"You were Pope Clement the Seventh."

"Yep. Quite the moderniser I was, within the context of the Catholic Church."

She picks up my Marlboros, shakes one out, and lights it with the thin slab of German steel I bought in Chiba in the 1980s. She blows out a huge plume of smoke, then says, "I'm a Catholic, you know that?"

"Of course I didn't know that. It's not on your LinkedIn page. But so what?"

"It's OK, I'm quite wishy-washy. But I could find it challenging to my faith to have a modern writer of historical novels sitting in front of me claiming to have been the holy father nearly five hundred years ago."

"What, it offends you?"

"No. Well yes, technically, it should do. I'm just not sure what to make of you. I mean, what would make you want to say that?"

"Because it's true," I say, looking at my watch. It's forty-two minutes since I pinned myself to the table. I stand up. "Let's take a look at my hand."

In the kitchen, I unwrap my hand, and run it under the cold tap. I dry it off on more kitchen paper, and hold it up in front of her, turning it back and forth, wiggling my fingers. On the palm, there is no sign of a wound. On the back of my hand, there is a thin red line, maybe a millimetre wide, about two centimetres long. On a non-Immortal, it could be a scar from a very minor injury a week ago, maybe picking blackberries. She sighs.

"Right." She takes my hand, and examines it closely. She goes to touch the remains of the wound, then pauses. "May I?" I nod. She rubs at it, tentatively at first, then she gently scrapes at it with her thumbnail. It doesn't come off, like I think she suspects it will.

"Not fake," I say, giving it a good hard rub. "But take a photo of it now, and look at it again in another hour. It'll be gone completely by then."

"You know, I think I will." We walk back onto the terrace, where she picks up her phone, takes a photo of the back of my hand, and puts it down again. We sit. More wine, more cigarettes.

"And watch my hands as we talk, just in case I do some sleight of hand and wipe off the wound."

"I'll be vigilant," she laughs. "But let's stay off the holy father for now."

"OK."

"So, take two," I say. "This is when I will be trying my damnedest to—"

"Why?" she interrupts loudly.

"Why? Why what?"

"Why are you two thousand years old?"

"I don't know."

"You — you don't know? Haven't you ever wondered?" I gave her a very, very old-fashioned look.

"Of course I have. It's the Holy Grail for us, finding out why we are like we are. Ever since science has been in any way a helpful thing, we've used the fuck out of it to find out who the hell we are. The first useful microscope ever was built by us, did you know that?"

"Um…"

"Of course you didn't know that. And although we didn't actually invent electron microscopes and gas chromatography, we were instrumental in making sure plenty of funding went to their development. Trouble is, we still have no idea why we are like we are. We have a couple of theories, obviously."

"Which are?"

"Pretty science fiction-y, mostly. One of my favourites is that we're a beta version of a next generation homo sapiens."

"A beta version? Why would—"

I laugh, probably not convincingly. "We are sterile. We can't have children. And there's not much point in evolving into a new race if you can't reproduce. Hence beta. Gotta go back to the lab for more work."

"You can't… hang on." She sits back in her chair and runs her fingers through her hair. Then she laughs and says, "No, it wouldn't make sense for you to be able to recreate if you live so long. The gene pool would get very muddy. I'm assuming you can't breed with non-Immortals too."

"Yes."

"Funny, that."

"Yes."

"And your DNA?"

"Standard. Nothing out of the ordinary at all, though we don't suffer from any genetic faults. And our genetic ancestry is a standard spread as well. I'm mostly Celtic, but I've also got some Northern German genes."

"Any other options? Aliens, for instance?" She's on the verge of taking the piss, but I'm playing it straight.

"Nothing of extraterrestrial origin, as far as we can tell."

"You'll have scanned yourselves with all the best diagnostic technology science can invent."

"Yes. We are, at a molecular level, human. We have human DNA, our anatomy and physiology are precisely the same."

"But Immortal."

"Yes. Well, no. We can die. But we're tough to kill, we come back from very bad injuries." I hold up my hand.

"Do you all look the same age?" She asks. "You say you're seventy-three, though you could pass for sixty. Surely having a... well, pardon me, but... if you're going to live for two thousand years... why don't you have a fit, twenty-five-year-old body?"

So I tell her about The Sleep, about how we rejuvenate ourselves every sixty or so years. She lights a cigarette off the butt of the last one and asks me to go through that bit again.

An hour later, we take a break. I cook some pork ravioli and serve it with some salad leaves, sliced tomatoes and roughly torn basil. As we eat it in the kitchen, I ask her about herself.

"I grew up in Napoli, Rione Sanita," she says.

"Cool part of town, I like it round there. Did you adopt a skull in the Fontanelle?"

"The pezzentelle? Of course."

"Big, middle class Catholic family? Lots of brothers and sisters?"

"Yep, two older brothers, two younger sisters. And my parents, and my Momma's Poppa and my Poppa's Momma living with us. Big household. Momma's family ran a couple of food places, so we always ate very well."

"And Naples is a very good place to eat. It's a great city."

"Yeah, it is. It's rough and ready, and it has its edges, but I love it."

"Always found the people there to be kind and generous myself," I say with a smile. "So what got you into journalism?"

"Poppa wrote for magazines and newspapers. It was all I ever wanted to do."

"And Saluti?" I ask, nodding at the magazine, "How long have you been there?"

"Eight years as a staff writer."

There's a couple of minutes' silence as we eat and drink, then once we're both finished, I nod toward the terrace. She smiles, and says, "OK then."

Back in our seats, she says, "OK then, let's get back to these two thousand-year-old people."

"OK."

"How many are there of you?"

"Last I heard, which was a few years ago, nine thousand, four hundred and twenty-two. There may be more unaccounted for, but VVO seem pretty sure they've been in contact with every Immortal in the world."

"And do you ever die?"

"Yes. Immortals have drowned, been beheaded, burnt at the stake, even been nuked in Hiroshima. I am slightly out of the loop, because I avoid VVO, but the last time I spoke about this with one of them he reckoned a hundred or so of us have died or been killed in the last two thousand years."

"So that, coupled with the fact that you can't reproduce, means there's only ever a finite number of you."

"Yes."

"Are you all white?"

"No, not at all. The race demographic among us is pretty much the same as it is with mortals."

"How do you recognise each other? I mean, you can't just go around telling people you're hundreds or thousands of years old and hoping one of them says 'Ooh, me too'. Is there...?" And she suddenly giggles. "Do you have a secret handshake?"

"Very funny. It's been touch and go over the centuries, but we have a well-established network around the world these days, with or without VVO. The digital age has made it much easier for us. Plus, some Immortals can Sense other Immortals."

"Sense?" She's clearly heard my spoken capital letter.

"Yeah, they can feel if another Immortal is nearby. I can't, but about ten or fifteen per cent of us can. It can be quite unreliable, but those who can Sense can have a range of up to about a hundred metres. Some can even tell what gender the Immortal they're Sensing is. When we have an Immortals-only party, there's always a Senser on the door." I laugh.

"OK. That makes, well, sense."

"You almost sound like you're starting to believe me."

"Of course not. You are, clearly, making it all up, but I'm suspending my disbelief for the moment, because it's a fascinating subject, and I'm loving how much you're sticking to your story. You've clearly worked out all the details."

"Thank you. I think."

"So what has this Very Very Old organisation done to annoy you?"

I sigh. "A couple of things. They had a hand, for instance, in the execution of a friend of mine, a mortal friend, back in 1663. They could quite easily have saved him, but instead they allowed him to die. I was, officially, a VVO agent at the time, but after he was killed, I walked away from them. Since then, I've done my best to avoid them, though lately they've come calling every few years."

"Why?"

"They don't like the amount of true, yet unverifiable historical details I put in my stories. It makes them nervous. It makes them think mortals will guess that I'm an Immortal."

"But that's dumb, surely that wouldn't be reason for any non-Immortals to think you're so old."

"You'd think so. But VVO are nothing if not cautious." I tell her about the conversations with Joseph Green and Zeynep Aksoy and some others over the years. I also make it clear that the mess that was made of the publication of *Lowonida*, not to mention its reception, is almost definitely down to skulduggery on the part of VVO.

"Yes," she says with a smile, "I can see how that would annoy you."

"You still have no doubt that I'm making this all up, right?"

"Look, I'm sorry, but there is no such thing as a human being who lives for over two thousand years. However, it's very entertaining. It's, well, as immersive as one of your books. I still think it's because you're trying out a new plot you're working up, and at the same time getting a bit of publicity so you can help the sales of *Lowonida*. Is that even close?"

"No," I say, lighting another cigarette.

"OK," she says with a sigh. "Tell me more. Tell me more stuff from two thousand years of life." And so I do.

An hour later, I hold up my left hand again, showing her the unblemished back and front. She takes it with a pinch of salt, even after comparing it with the photo on her phone.

I've been laying it on thick, telling her the real stories behind many of my novels, trying to drown her in details that could only mean what I'm saying is true.

There are, of course, a few things I veer away from. One is the names or identities of any other Immortals, especially the few who are celebs. I also don't mention our four Long Laboratories. But the rest of what I tell her is authentic and detailed.

Somewhere near four p.m., we stop again, and have Aperol cocktails and nuts and olives, and we talk about films and music and books and clothes and restaurants, and sometimes, it's just like we're acquaintances having a catch up.

Then it's her turn. She hammers the questions at me relentlessly, almost as if I'm a hostile witness in a courtroom. Sometimes she tries to trip me up by going back to something I've said earlier and asking me about it again; she takes copious notes. I tell the absolute truth, I don't trip up on anything. After about an hour of this, she comes to a halt. She drains her glass, and tops it up again, then lights another cigarette; between us we've killed three bottles of wine, and we're on our second pack of Marlboros. There is silence for a minute. Then she says, "So, what you're basically saying is that you're at least two thousand years old, as are another nine thousand plus of you?"

"In a nutshell, yes. Have I convinced you?"

She sighs. "Look, Mr Mitchell. I have had a very entertaining day. For the last, what, five or six hours, I've been in a science fiction novel, or maybe magical realism. It's been really quite exciting, despite the stupid stuff with the knife. But I still don't... I can't believe, without, you know, scientific evidence..."

"There is one more way I can, well, if not prove it, at least make it beyond any reasonable doubt. It'll take a month or two, but it is doable."

"How?" she asks. And I tell her.

She leaves twenty minutes later; we hug, and kiss each other's cheeks at my front door and she thanks me for a memorable day. I watch from the balcony as she exits the building, and walks up the street and out of sight.

The interview is, of course, spiked. A week after Chiara and I speak, the magazine editor calls my agent and tells him that, due to scheduling difficulties, it won't now be appearing in the August issue as was planned; she's not sure when it will. My agent pesters me to know what it is we talked about, what I said to piss them off so badly, but I keep my mouth shut. VVO have flexed their muscles again.

A fortnight after the interview, I fly to New York. Two months later, after Sleeping in my place in Manhattan, I return to Rome under my new identity, Pavel Krebowski, staying in an anonymous two-star hotel. I've brought with me the letter Chiara Congliani gave me just before leaving the rented apartment, that she wrote to herself, and I partially dictated.

It says, "Chiara, this man, who you knew as Geoffrey Mitchell, is at least two thousand years old. You last saw him before he Slept, and you thought he looked sixty, although his passport said he was seventy-three. He has now Slept, but he's still the same man. This should help convince you that he is who he says he is." Underneath it is a series of strings of numbers, some codes she thought up on the spot; PINs maybe, or old telephone numbers or birth dates of friends or loved ones, she never told me, though she took several photos of the sheet with her phone before she handed it over to me. There's also a good quality print from my right thumb; I inked it with a magic marker, and pressed it against the paper when she'd finished writing it. There's space beside the thumbprint for another.

So I sit in a cafe opposite the Saluti offices and I wait for Chiara Congliani to come out.

Tiernan Ogue in Wexford

"Ladies and Gentlemen, please welcome to the stage…
Corvid!"

And the crowd goes wild.

Later, backstage, I'm loafing on a sofa necking ice
cold lager, stripped down to teeshirt and trunks; it was
hot in there, the smallest venue we've played in years,
and the latest iterations of our costumes, though light as
a feather, do nothing to keep one cool when one is
leaping about a stage screaming one's head off.

Chaz, the lead guitarist, is at the bar chatting with
bassist Frank; they're both drinking Vodka Redbulls.
Jim, drums, is sitting at a table, a bacon cheeseburger
and a pint of Stoli-Boli on the go, swiping through the
photo feed on an iPad. Alison, decks and keyboards, is
nowhere to be seen; she's probably in a band SUV on
the way back to The Crow's Nest with Dinah, her wife.
Recovering alcoholics, they have a longstanding
agreement with the rest of us that they don't join in
after-show shenanigans. Fat Freddie Scat, our manager,
is hovering nearby. I sign the record cover being
brandished at me by a skinny, gender fluid Gen Z,

wondering how they got in, and if they even know what a record is, then let Fat Freddie chase them away.

"So, you set for the morning?" he says, sitting down on the sofa beside me, fat cheeks puffing out with the effort.

"Yep. TV Éireann, Good Morning Ireland with Francie Donald, live at seven-forty-five. Gotta be at the studios by seven. I'm set."

"Good. You and Jim this time."

"I know, I know. I may be a lead singer, but I'm not stupid."

"Good. Make sure you've done up your fly. And either wear sunglasses, or don't get caught looking at her tits. Though you'd be an eejit not to," he adds with a lascivious grin. "They are fabulous."

At seven thirty the next morning, Jim and I are sitting in the green room at the TV Éireann studios on Trinity Street in Wexford town. Jim is looking a tad bleary, his shaven pate sweaty. Last I saw of him as I left The Crow Bar at about midnight, he was downing a pint of champagne as fast as he could, a spliff the size of a leg tucked behind his ear, a wrap of powder and a rolled-up tenner on the bar before him. Still wearing some of last night's black and grey stage clothes, though fortunately not his mask, he's nursing a TV Éireann pint mug of café latte. I'm in a slim black suit, a white teeshirt, white pointed patent leather shoes and dark glasses with white frames. My hair, a close crop, is black on the left, white on the right.

The huge flat screen on the green room wall is showing what's going on in the studio. Francie Donald, fifty-five-ish, maternally beautiful, dazzling white teeth, ash blonde bob, cold green eyes behind spectacles, is pretending to sympathise with some codger who's Skyped in to whinge about… something or other. Francie is wearing a white blouse and does, indeed, appear to have fabulous tits. Then there's an ad break, and a runner appears at the green room door, consulting a clipboard.

"Mr Ogue? Mr Reeves? Can you come to the studio now please? You're on next."

We rise and follow him to the huge squashy sofa opposite Francie Donald's huge squashy armchair. We shake hands with her and sit.

"Hello, Mr Ogue, Mr Reeves. Lovely to meet you. Can I address you by your Christian names?"

"I'm not a Christian, but you can use my first name if you like," Jim says. Her smile falters microscopically, then is re-applied.

"Ah, OK, Mr Reeves. It's Jim, isn't it? Jim Reeves? Any relation?" she jokes.

"To who?" Jim asks.

"Erm, Jim Reeves? He was a country singer in the '50s and '60s."

"Never heard of him," Jim answers, deadpan. Inside, I'm giggling.

A guy in a headset with a clipboard says "Sixty seconds, Francie."

She nods and says, "So we'll start with a little clip from the show last night, and have a brief chat about that, then the tour with –" She consults her notes. "- Belle Epoque and Trudna... erm, how do you say this? Trudna Mel... Milo..."

"Trood Na Mwah Dyesh," Jim says, pronouncing the band's name phonetically.

"Trudna Młodzież are Polish. It means Difficult Youth," I add. Jim has become good mates with them during the European tour, and learnt how to say their name. I've been able to speak Polish for centuries, though Corvid are under the impression I once had a girlfriend from Kraków.

"Ah, OK, Trood Na Mwah Dyesh. Thanks, fellows, that could have been embarrassing on air!" she laughs, and scribbles a note on her clipboard. "Then we'll have a few words about the band in general and the new album, and finish up with a quick Skype-In."

"Skype-In? What's that?" I ask.

"Oh, it's just a few members of the public, they'll just ask you who your favourite band is, or what you like to eat after a show, nothing contentious. We weed out the, you know, weirdos."

"Lady, we are the weirdos," Jim and I chorus. It's the fade out line from our debut single, *Black Wing*. We look at each other and burst out laughing, just as the guy in the headset says, "Quiet on set, please. Twenty seconds."

Then it's a spoken countdown from ten to five, and a hand-signed countdown to zero, and the 'ON AIR' sign illuminates.

"Welcome back," says Francie Donald to a nearby camera, her image filling many of the ceiling and wall-mounted monitors. "Now, if you're a big fan of the opera, you might want to look away at this point. Last night, Wexford's National Opera House, just a few minutes away from here, had some very odd visitors. If you'd been in the vicinity, you may have been surprised to see loads of young people, all wearing, well, forty shades of black, many with crow masks, all streaming into the building. Now they weren't there to see an opera, oh no, they were there to see... well, let's take a look at this clip, shall we?"

We did, of course, make sure there was a film crew for this very special gig, and the clip that comes up on the monitors is part of their footage. Some twenty minutes into the first half of the show, we're doing *Where is the Glove?,* our fifteenth single, from *Kind of a Dark Outlook,* our seventh album. It's a nasty, thrashy, aggressive belter of a song, all minor chords played at supersonic speed by my rhythm guitar and Chaz's lead, and huge slabs of thunder from Alison's machines, Jim's drums and Frank's bass, as I grunt out the lyrics:-

And yet/still you try/to take away/the pride/the peace/the love.

Who do you think you are?/Where, indeed, is the glove?

And so on and so forth. It's one of my favourite songs of ours, one I wrote most of, and the clip they're showing is a good one, mostly wide-angle shots from up on the balcony, with the occasional close-up. The band is playing as tight as is possible; the light show is dazzling in its intensity; the crowd are having a wild time, jumping and screaming, moshing and singing. We look great, our crow masks shimmering with LEDs, my black and white cloak swooping and sweeping like wings. Chaz, Frank and I all have Phil Lynott style chrome scratch plates on our black gloss guitars, and they're superb for reflecting the lights back into the crowd. To be honest, it sends shivers down my spine, and I am almost disappointed when it ends.

"Wow," says Francie, as she reappears on the monitors. "Pretty intense stuff! That's a song called *Where is the Glove?*. It's from a band that call themselves Corvid. They're internationally famous, lead singer, Tiernan Ogue, and drummer, Jim Reeves, are local boys, and they're with us this morning. Welcome, lads, welcome to the show."

"Thanks, Francie," I say. Jim nods and smiles and sips from his coffee.

"So, Tiernan, can I ask you, why choose the Opera House of all places? I wouldn't have thought it was anywhere near big enough for a band of your stature."

"Well no, Francie, under normal circumstances, we tend to play huge venues, you know, stadiums, fifty, sixty thousand seaters. We headlined at the Stade De France in Paris a few weeks ago, and that's got a capacity of over eighty thousand. That's right, isn't it?" I say to Jim, who loves his stats.

"Eighty thousand, seven hundred and ninety-six, the night we played. Quite a place."

"Wow! So why our little Opera House? I'm not sure how many folks you can get in there, but I'm sure it's barely a fraction of that!"

"Seven hundred and seventy-four last night," Jim says.

"Yep, way smaller than usual," I say. "It was a free show for our Irish fan club, the Jayses, and we thought, what with two of the five of us coming from Wexford town, it'd be a great venue to do it in. It did take a certain amount of… negotiation with the management, but our fans are pretty respectful, really. They were never going to wreck the place, so we were able to secure it."

"And the tickets were free?"

"We did a lottery on our website a few months ago, thousands of people entered, and the seven hundred and seventy-four who came to see us last night were lucky enough to get free tickets. And they seemed to have a blast."

"They certainly seemed to be having a good time!" says Francie. She indicates a screen nearby showing ecstatic fans jumping up and down as a crane cam swoops along the front row.

"Indeed. We thought it'd be nice to give back something for all the support they've shown us over the years."

"And they're called the Jayses? Is that what you called them?" she asks, though it's quite clearly printed in large text on her clipboard.

"It's what they call themselves, not Jayses as in, you know, Jesus, but Jayses as in a double plural of Jay, which is, as I'm sure you know, a type of crow," says Jim. "Also, it wasn't us set up the fan club, they did."

"They're a great bunch," I say, "and we love their passion and enthusiasm. Lately, in between songs, they've started doing that weird Arabic ululating thing, it sounds great."

"Wow" she says, "Almost sounds like they're part of the band."

"Well, obviously we'd be nothing without our fans" I say.

"And there's a new album out?"

"Newish, it came out last month, on my birthday" I lie, "The eleventh of March. We've always released albums on someone in the band's birthday." Obviously, I have no idea when my actual date of birth some two thousand years ago is, but '11 MAR 1987' is what it says on my passport.

"And it's called *Cromwell's Crows*" she says, her voice suddenly going downbeat and serious. "Which is, if you'll excuse me, a bit of an odd name, is it not?"

"Not really. The Magpie, obviously my bird, my persona in the band, was known as Cromwell's Crow at one stage in Ireland. People thought Oliver Cromwell had brought them to Ireland with him, though in reality the first time they were recorded in Ireland was in 1676, and Cromwell had been and gone by then."

"So what's the album all about then?" she asks. She has a half smile on her face, and I am suddenly wary of this line of questioning.

"Well, if you take the title track, for instance, that's about occupation" I say, "About colonisation, about a people being taken over by another people, moved from their lands, killed and repressed, and indeed about the ecological destruction of territories. We do mention Cromwell, but we mostly use him as a metaphor."

"Really? I'm told there are lyrics in one of the other songs that seem to praise Cromwell's introduction of new, modern agricultural techniques to primitive Irish communities. Considering the evil, brutal violence Cromwell and his lot visited on the Irish, isn't that a bit of a contentious issue?"

"Yeah, you're right, especially if you take it out of context, as you're doing now," says Jim, "The song you're referring to is called *The Adventurer's Act*. And if you'd listened to it yourself, or your researcher had written you better notes –" He nods to her clipboard, "you'd know that the song is from the point of view of a captain in Cromwell's army, and he's feeling guilty about the fact that he's been given hundreds of acres of prime farmland the original Irish Catholic owners have been kicked off, and he's trying to justify his actions by referring to what he sees as the advantages the invasion has brought to Ireland. It's not us condoning what Cromwell did in Ireland at all."

"Oh, right," she says, "I'm sorry, I must get one of your fans in as a researcher! Anyway, moving on, you've just been touring Europe with two other heavy metal bands, Belle Epoque and - I must be careful to pronounce this right - Trudna Młodzież. How did that go?"

The interview goes on for another few minutes; there's a potted history of Corvid - formed in 2010 when we were still at Uni, same line-up throughout, nine albums, lots of singles, huge sales worldwide - but I let Jim do most of the talking. I'm pretty pissed off; there's no doubt in my mind that we've been set up, although not very well. The Cromwell stuff has been bubbling at a low level for a few weeks, ever since the album was released. Some literary prick on the radio tore into it the week after it came out. That had had limited exposure, but this is going to get to a much wider audience. This is, of course, good and bad. We'll get plenty of sales out of it, but we'll also be getting a very hard time from that section of the Irish population that doesn't want to talk about Cromwell.

We come to the Skype-In, the first one from a breathless woman fan who was there last night, and tells us it was the best gig she's ever been to. Her raven mask, representing Chaz, is pushed up onto the top of her head, looking like a witch's hat, suiting her goth makeup, black lace cloak and black back-combed hair perfectly. She signs off with a loud, 'Kronk'.

The next Skype comes from two women and two men, late twenties/early thirties, with their masks hanging round their necks. The men have hooded crow and rook masks, representing Jim and Frank, and the women have magpie and jackdaw ones, me and Alison. They weren't able to get tickets, and they want to know when we plan to play in Wexford again.

"I don't know, to be honest," and a sly idea comes into my head, "and I'm so sorry you didn't get to see us play last night, it was a stormer of a gig. But… look… I'll tell you what. We're playing Metalfezt in Dublin in October this year, how about Good Morning Ireland buys you tickets for that? VIP tickets, of course." Francie Donald's eyebrows jump off the top of her head. "They can drive you to Croke Park in a limo, give you all sorts of freebies and memorabilia, get you into the VIP area, maybe even film you, you know, for the website? I'd love to meet you in person before or after the show. How would that be, Francie?" Her face replaces the split screen shot of me and the goths, her eyebrows back in place.

"Yes, Mr Ogue, uh, Tiernan, that would be a grand idea. Why don't we do that? Please," she says to the delighted goths on the screen, bouncing up and down and hugging each other, ululating for all they're worth, "please leave names and contact details with a producer once we're finished here, and we can certainly do that."

The next Skype-In comes from some old git with a bee in his bonnet about all these terrible young folks with their black clothes and their noisy bands and isn't it awful and there was one with an upside down crucifix round their neck there in the video and shouldn't the authorities be doing something about it and isn't it Godless and they call themselves Jayzuz which you must agree is sacrilegious and -

"Well, I'm afraid that's all the time the boys here have," Francie says, cutting him off before Jim or I have had the chance to say anything to him. "It's just coming up to eight o'clock. We'll take a quick commercial break then go over to Dublin for the news. See you after that for the last segment of the show, when we'll be talking to Zara Devine about her new book about the wild flowers of Ireland. Oh, and don't forget, we'll be broadcasting Good Morning Ireland from Cork next week." Her smile disappears completely as the 'ON AIR' light goes out.

"Ye might have told me you were going to do that!" she snaps at me, "Making us buy VIP tickets for one of your little concerts! Driving a bunch of feckin' eejits up to Dublin in a limo indeed!"

"Little concert? The Croker seats eighty-two thousand people!" Jim says. I add "You might have told us you were going to bring up the Cromwell stuff. I don't remember you saying anything about it before we went live, do you? Besides, we can comp you the tickets if money is a problem. We can afford it." Jim sniggers at my side.

She harrumphs, then gets up and walks off the set. The studio floor manager looks after her with some concern.

"Don't worry," I say, standing as the runner gestures for us to come with him, "I'm sure she'll be back before the news is over. She's a consummate professional."

A couple of years ago, we had a huge, very public Twitter row about one's duty to pay one's income tax with a certain Irish rock god, and we got ourselves banned from Dublin's Windmill Lane studios while we were recording our eighth album *The Song Remains Insane*, so, after de-camping to an equally good recording facility in West London to finish it off, we built our own studio complex in the countryside in Wexford. It is toward that establishment, The Crow's Nest, that we are heading now. In the car, Jim and I bitch about Francie Donald, ignoring our phones, Fat Freddie ringing us both several times.

When we arrive at The Crow's Nest, we are, of course, bollocked by Freddie; he watched the interview over breakfast with the rest of the band and he's not impressed with the Cromwell bit. After a load of passive aggressive whinging delivered in his Cork accent, I shout, 'Enough!' and he shuts up. We have work to do.

In 2018, we did something we swore we'd never do, we released *Eating Crow, The Very Best of Corvid*. A remastered collection of all twenty of our singles in chronological order, it sold incredibly well, over a million in its first six months. Fat Freddie's idea, it made us a huge amount of money. The band, however, insisted on one sticking point.

Our condition upon which the release of *Eating Crow* depended, was that there'd be a *Volume Two* a couple of years later, a double album this time. *Disc One* would be a set of remixes from some of the best young producers in the business; we've chosen a dozen of them, and they're coming to The Crow's Nest to do the work over the next couple of weeks. It's a bit of an odd arrangement, but we are a very hands-on band, we like to oversee the production of our music as much as we can.

Disc Two would be a rather different beast. Over the years, we have, as all bands do, accumulated a vast archive of recordings that have never been released; demos, songs that never got finalised, alternate mixes, different lyrics, Jim and Frank trying new rhythm patterns, Alison messing about with looped up samples and keyboard sequences, sometimes just me on an acoustic guitar trying out lyrical ideas, sometimes Chaz bending the bejasus out of his guitar strings – there are hundreds of hours of audio. So that second CD will be made up of a carefully chosen musical collage taken from that unreleased archive, roughly ninety minutes long. This is what we've been busying ourselves with over the last few days, cutting, pasting, syncing and remastering.

So, at about nine o'clock, after arming ourselves with various beverages and snacks, we install ourselves on the sofas by the mixing desk. At the controls are producer, Pete McNally, a Wicklow wideboy, and engineer, Kevin Strange, a taciturn Belfast man. They've been with us for years, they know us inside out, and we trust them implicitly to do a good job.

"So, yesterday" Kev says, "While you lot were leaping about the Opera House like a bunch of feckin' eejits, we finalised the first rough mix of *Disc Two*. Everything's been more or less equalised, all the BPMs and keys are nice and neat, we just need you guys to give it one last listen, and then we can render the whole thing. Starts with a cleaned up version of your original demo of *A Crow and a Baby*, our second single, a cover of the Human League song from some twenty years earlier, "and blends, rather wonderfully, I have to admit, into a mash of *With Wings Pressed Back* and an early acoustic of *Europe Under its Wing*. Here, have a listen." And he clicks a mouse.

Three hours later, we are in complete agreement, *Disc Two* is ready to go to press, so to speak. We congratulate ourselves with high fives and clinks of glasses of juice and mugs of tea and coffee.

"So you lot can all fuck off now," says Fat Freddie.

"Charming," says Alison, opening a can of Perrier. "We're only the poor feckers who made the music in the first place."

"He's so fuckin' ungrateful," says Chaz, lighting a cigar.

"What about the remix stuff?" I ask. "Do we have anyone coming today?"

"Not today," Freddie says. "Those two young hip-hop lads from London, Flare In Soho they call themselves, they're having a go at *The Scavenger and the Scholar* on Thursday, and that mad German techno woman from Berghain is coming on Friday. Sie hat mir erzählt, dass sie unsere Musik viel sexyer machen kann."

"I never knew you spoke German, Freddie," I say. "My days of calling you an uneducated idiot are certainly coming to a middle."

"Oh, do fuck off, there's a good chap," Freddie says with a grin. "In fact, all of you, fuck off. Go off and do… whatever it is you do when you're not making me a rich man. But be back here bright and early the day after tomorrow, or I'll have your balls for bowties."

"Me too?" Alison laughs.

"Especially you," says Freddie.

Upstairs at The Crow's Nest, we have a suite each; fully kitted out in luxury hotel style, it's where we stay when we're deep into the intricate process of making an album. We have quite a good work ethic when we're in this mode, and although some of us use a certain amount of pharmaceutical help, we work very hard on our recording sessions, usually knocking off the whole album in about two months. There's a well-stocked and equipped kitchen/diner up there too; we're all quite good cooks, though we do tend to hire a chef when we're here for more than a couple of days. It is in my room, Pica Pica, that I change into my black and white cycling skins. The rest of the band have been trying to get me to appear on stage in this sort of outfit for years, maybe even cycling on from the wings on one of my bikes - think of the sponsorship, they say - but it kind of wouldn't really work; I can't imagine The Jayses would be massively impressed. In the kitchen, I fill a steel bottle with water.

Downstairs, I unhitch my favourite bike, the black Venge Pro, from its wall mounted hanger in the lobby and turn the GPS tracker on my iPhone on and put it into its slot on the crossbar. This last has been a bit of a sticking point; Fat Freddie used to get very worried when I went out on the bike, even following me at one stage in his vast black Range Rover, until I lost him in the winding back streets of New Ross. He was, of course, terrified of his meal ticket getting knocked off his bike by '...Some twat in a Beamer...', and only finding out about it off the evening news. So we came to a compromise; I turn the FindMy function on when I go for one of my spins, he shuts the fuck up about me getting killed.

Jim is off to see his family in Galway, I wave goodbye to him as I pass him on the drive, climbing into his car. Chaz, Frank and I are all staying here for the next few days. Chaz and Frank are both keen birdwatchers, and are off to the river by Tintern, which is excellent for waders at this time of the year, while I plan to do a fifty-kilometre cycling/exploring circuit each day. Alison and Dinah have already disappeared; they keep themselves to themselves when the band isn't at work, and are probably already on the road to Ballincrea, where they have a house. Freddie is nowhere to be seen either; chances are he's off to Dublin to either set up our next few gigs or sell his grandmother.

It never takes me long to settle into a rhythm when I'm on the bike. Today, my body responds to it immediately, and before I've completed a kilometre, I'm in the zone.

Sadly, this zen-like calm doesn't last long. About ten minutes out from The Crow's Nest, just after I've turned onto a side road, a black Lexus SUV starts to overtake me, then the side door slides open, and an automatic is pointed at my face by a guy in a black hoodie with one of those Occupy style Guy Fawkes masks covering his face. I glance backwards, thinking that maybe I could slam on the brakes and double back, but there's a motorcycle coming up behind, and the pillion passenger, with a black full-face crash helmet, is pointing another handgun at me. The guy in the Lexus waves a hand, indicating that I need to stop. Given the gun he's pointing at me is one of the most powerful handguns on the market, and could do a lot of damage to even a tough motherfucker like me, I comply.

The guy from the SUV and the passenger from the motorbike pull me from my bike, yank my helmet off and handcuff me. The phone is pulled from the crossbar, stomped to bits underfoot and kicked into the water at the bottom of the ditch at the side of the road, the bike and helmet thrown over the hedge, then I'm shoved into the SUV, hands grabbing me and pushing me to the floor. A cloth bag is thrown over my head with a drawstring pulled tight at my neck, the handcuffs are attached to what feels like some sort of metal loop, then the door slams shut, and we're moving.

I don't panic, I've been in worse situations than this before, much worse. Instead, I concentrate on counting turns, estimating time and distance travelled, trying to keep a good idea of where we're going. I know the backroads of this county intimately, I've been cycling them for years, so when we pull up twenty minutes later, after turning off a road and bumping along what feels like a badly maintained track, I'm pretty sure we're at the old Bolger place, a disused, abandoned farm. Its buildings are invisible from the road, but I know it from when we were playing with our new toy, a professional level camera drone, a few months ago. Then, from a vantage point in a car park a kilometre or so away, Kev had flown it low over the boarded up farmhouse, up and down the weed strewn farmyard, and in and out of some of the dilapidated, collapsing sheds and barns, the band clustered around a monitor, watching what the drone was seeing through its four cameras. I'm confident we're no more than eight km from The Crow's Nest.

The door slides open, I'm hauled to my feet, and manhandled out of the Lexus. The ground underfoot is uneven, I can feel weeds and mud under my cycling shoes. A hand grasps each of my elbows, and I'm marched about twenty metres, then I hear a door creak open, and the acoustics tell me we're indoors. I'm pushed down onto a chair, my ankles are attached with what I can tell from the sound are cable ties, my hands are uncuffed, then locked again, this time behind the back of the chair. Then the hood is pulled off.

I appear to be in a kitchen, an empty, disused one, no cooker, no fridge, other than some shabby built in cupboards; there's no furniture save my chair and a bar stool nearby. The window is boarded up, the only illumination coming from a bright white portable strip light standing upright in a corner, battery powered, I presume. Five people stand in front of me, in black jeans, black hoodies and Guy Fawkes masks. I think it's one woman and four men. One of the men, the one I assume to be the leader, is standing slightly in front of the others, the gun in his gloved right hand. On the floor nearby, there's a black rucksack, a laptop, a GoPro camera and what I'm fairly sure is a satellite phone.

"What the actual fuck?" I ask, quite reasonably.

"What the fuck do you think, asshole? You've been kidnapped," the man with the gun says. He has a Dublin accent, Southside, middle class, nearly posh.

"Well, now, what would you want to do something as fucking stupid as that for?"

In two strides he's right in front of me, smacking the barrel of the gun across my face. My nose breaks noisily, blood splashes us both and starts to pour down my face from both nostrils. One of the others lets out an involuntary gasp.

"You don't get to talk to me like that. You get to shut the fuck up, and hope your crappy little band mates want you back enough to pay a fucking big ransom."

"Wow," I say. "You mean business."

"You better believe it, dickhead. So I don't want to hear any more shit out of you. In fact..." And he goes to the rucksack and pulls out a roll of bandage and another of duct tape.

I can guess what he wants to do with them, but I need to be able to keep talking, so I say, "My nose is full of blood, it'll be one solid scab soon and I'll only be able to breathe through my mouth. If you gag me, I'll suffocate and die. If I suffocate and die, your bargaining chip is gone, plus you get done for murder when they finally catch you."

He pauses. One of the other figures, a man, speaks.

"He's right, Jos - um, Number One. He needs to be alive for the, you know, ransoming." A Wexford accent, also middle class.

Joseph, for that is what I'm now assuming the leader's name to be, turns quickly and hisses at his teammate.

"Shut up, Number Four! I do the talking, like we agreed." He turns back to me. "Right, no gag. But every time you speak out of turn, I will hurt you. Club you in the face with my gun, kick you in the balls, maybe a good solid gut punch. OK?"

I say nothing.

"OK?" he repeats.

"OK," I say.

"So," says Joseph, "First thing we need to do is let your lot know what's going on. Number Two, the camera." The short one at the end of the line, the one I assume to be a woman, picks up the GoPro, and hands it to Joseph. He clips it to the front of his hoody, pointing it at me.

"So," he says, "we're going to record you pleading for your life, then we're going to upload it and send your band the link. If they haven't paid us within twenty-four hours, we put a bullet in your head and leave your body in the middle of the M11. What do you think of that?"

"When did you come up with this plan, in the pub last night?" This time, he gut punches me as promised, but I see it coming and tense my stomach muscles. It hurts, but there's no lasting damage. I gasp and cough for effect.

"I mean," I continue, after spluttering convincingly for about thirty seconds, "given the shitty internet speeds around these parts, how the frig are you going to upload it without it timing out? And, for that matter, how do you plan to cover your tracks so no one can trace it back here?"

"Number Three," Joseph says, "show him."

Number Three, a bulky male, holds up the satellite phone. "The equivalent of 5G. Super fast," he says in a bland Northern Irish accent, maybe West Belfast. Then he opens the laptop and spins it round so I can see the screen. Some sort of video editing software app is open, plus what appears to be a Dark Web window.

"Upload to the net through several grey accounts scattered around the world," he says. "I've got the maaaaaad skillz." He giggles, then gets silenced by a glance from Joseph.

"Any other problems?" he asks, and I can hear the smirk behind the mask.

"Well, yes," I say ""How do my lot let you know that they agree? That they'll give you the money?"

"By posting the phrase, 'Tiernan Ogue's safety' on the blog page of the official Corvid website. Then we'll give them details about how to hand the ransom over."

"Well, speaking of which, how do they get the money to you? Not cash, obviously, way too risky. Not a direct transfer to some anonymous off-shore account. Even Bitcoins can be traceable. How then?"

This unsettles him.

"Actually, it will be Bitcoins, to an account we control. We can then –"

"What, all of you?" I ask.

"What? What do you mean all of us?" Joseph says.

"I mean, do all of you control this Bitcoin account? Do you all have access to it? You know, usernames and passwords. Do you?" I ask, looking up at each of the others in turn. "Will you all be able to get into the account? Get your, whatever, hundreds of thousands of euro each? Or are you trusting Joseph here to split the proceeds evenly?"

Numbers Three and Four look at each other. The other two look at Joseph.

"Everyone will get an equal share," he says. "We've all worked equally hard on this project, we're all in it together. And now it's your turn to contribute."

"Ah, time for my closeup, is it? Let's have a look at the script, then."

"Script? You don't need a script!" Joseph snaps. "You will tell them that you've been taken, that unless they pay us five million euro, your head will be blown off, on screen, and that they have one hour to agree and twelve hours to pay up. And no police. Simple."

"OK," I say brightly, though I can't believe how amateur this operation sounds. "Let's do it. I'm not that interested in dying just yet."

Joseph fires up the GoPro, points it at me, zooming in a little. Then he nods.

"Morning, folks," I say "I've got a bit of a situation here, and I need your help. I seem to have got myself kidnapped by five people. They —"

"Stop!" says Joseph. "No numbers. Just the main message. Start again."

"OK. Sorry." I take a breath, and start again. "Morning, folks. I've got a bit of a situation here, and I need your help. I seem to have got myself kidnapped by... some people. They want you lot to scrape together five million euro and hand it over to them, or I get shot through the head. If you agree to this, you have one hour to put text up on the blog page of our website saying... saying... what was it again?"

"Oh, for fuck's sake!" Joseph shouts. "'Tiernan Ogue's safety'. Start again!"

I run through it again, ending with "...Tiernan Ogue's safety. Um, I think that's it, I don't want to drone on about it, but please, get your wallets out, especially you, Charles. Oh, and not a word to the police. Hope to hear from you soon as possible, cheers, bye." I pause for a few seconds. "How was that?"

"That was just fine," Joseph sneers. "We'll edit it into shape and upload it. Number Five, stay with him. Shoot him if he so much as twitches. The rest of you, next door." He picks up the laptop, satphone and rucksack and walks past me, followed by Two, Three and Four. I hear a door behind me open and close.

Number Five, small, skinny, with a nervous disposition that's obvious even with the mask on, hoists himself into a sitting position on the dusty counter, pulls his gun out of a pocket, then puts it down on the counter beside him. I can see it's a Taipan 360. From China, it's one of the cheapest automatics on the market and is prone to jamming and overheating, and is difficult to reload quickly. It also ejects spent cases directly upwards, which can result in hot pieces of brass landing about one's person.

"What, Joseph didn't trust you with a proper gun?" I ask, nodding at the Taipan.

"Shut the fuck up. You heard Number One, any guff from you and –"

"He couldn't have left the automatic with you? Lovely gun, that, big and dependable and accurate, not like that pissy little -"

"Shut. The fuck. Up! Or I'll –"

"Shoot me? Blow your hostage away? I'm sure he'd just love that."

"Did you not hear the bit where I told you to shut the fuck up? One more word and I will gag you, nose full of blood or not. Don't forget, we don't actually need you alive any more, we have you recorded, they're probably uploading it as we speak." I'm not so sure of this; from behind the door, I can hear raised voices. I can't tell what's being said, but it doesn't sound like there's a cordial atmosphere in that room. I presume

Number Four is being given a bollocking for accidentally naming Joseph.

"OK, but two things you need to think about; he's Number One, you're Number Five. There are at least three people in your Scooby Gang he considers more important than you, not including himself. Plus, of the two of us in this room, I have a way bigger chance of walking out of this situation alive than you do, OK?" He jumps off the counter at this, and, like his boss, strikes me across the face with the gun. I make sure I go over with a crash, shouting and squealing, landing awkwardly on my left arm. I feel the clunk and click of my thumb partially dislocating. The door bangs open as Five goes to hit me again, and Joseph strides in.

"Five!" Joseph shouts. "Stop it!" Five stops. Joseph shoves him towards the door. "Give Number Two your gun, go next door and calm the fuck down!" Five starts to say something, but Joseph shouts, "Now!" at him. Five hands the gun over to the woman while Joseph rights my chair.

"Now you," Joseph hisses at me, "Not a fucking word. OK? Number Two, watch him like a hawk." She nods. Numbers Three and Four go back into the next room and Joseph follows them, closing the door. Number Two sits on the bar stool, maybe two metres from where I sit.

"So, what do you want to talk about then?" I say.

"For fuck's sake, you heard Number One. Shut up!" Her accent is the same as Joseph's, middle class, South Dublin.

"Yeah, Number One, Joseph, he's such a professional, isn't he? Can't even stop his own people from shouting out his name."

"Shut the fuck up! No more!"

"OK," I say, "OK." And I go silent.

For the next hour or so, we sit in silence; from the next room I can hear occasional voices, including, about forty-five minutes in, Joseph saying 'Yesssss!', presumably at the news that the money is on the way. A moment later I hear the door open, Number Two looks up and nods, then the door closes again. My eyes closed, I am as still and quiet as I can be, just shifting every now and then, as if to stretch aching muscles. In reality, I'm working at the joint at the base of my left thumb, pushing and pulling at it with my right hand, doing my best to get the whole digit to dislocate completely. It is, of course, extremely painful. And then, with a final clunk I have to cough to cover the sound of, it finally pops. Just after it does, I hear a sound outside the kitchen window. It may be a dog, it maybe be a fox, it may be a rat, but I need to make sure my guard doesn't hear it.

"Fuck this, I'm bored, let's have a chat," I say loudly, sliding my left hand painfully out of its handcuff, but keeping it behind my back. "Tell me what you're going to do with your share of the money. Assuming Joseph remembers to give it to you."

"I thought I told you to stay quiet," she says.

"I mean, he's not exactly a professional, is he? He thinks he's got this well-oiled kidnap machine up and running, but he's made fundamental mistake after fundamental mistake. This is his first ever kidnap, that's very obvious."

"What do you mean, fundamental mistakes? This whole operation was planned to the millimetre, to the nanosecond. We've been watching you for days, we know exactly what your mid-morning routine is, the way we grabbed you was textbook. We will get the money, and we will get away. And anyway, what do you know about kidnapping? How the fuck does some soft middleclass pop star who dresses up like a fucking bird every night and jumps about screaming and shouting for a living know anything at all about kidnapping? Eh? Answer me that. I'm sure if you'd been kidnapped before, you'd have written one of your piss poor songs about it."

"I do, indeed, have experience of kidnapping. I've seen it up close, I've seen professionals at work, and I can tell you, your whole enterprise is doomed to failure." This is no less than the truth, though I don't tell her when the last time I was involved in a kidnapping was, partly because she doesn't need to know my age, but mostly because I, and the rest of the FBI, failed to get the victim returned safely during those terrible few weeks in 1932 in New Jersey; we weren't dealing with professionals then either. "Also, one or more of you lot will be dead before this day is over, and I will almost definitely survive."

She picks up the gun and points it at me.

"And if I were to pull the trigger right now?" she says, a sneer in her voice.

"Nothing would happen. The safety catch is on."

She looks down at the gun, and that's when I explode out of the chair, diving across the kitchen, grabbing at her legs as they dangle off the barstool. My left hand isn't working perfectly, but I still manage to yank Number Two onto the floor. She lands awkwardly on her arse, the gun falling from her hand. We both dive sideways, scrabbling for it as it skitters across the floor, but I'm slightly faster, so, when the door opens and Joseph bursts in again, it is to find me sitting back against the cupboard under the counter, the chair still attached to my feet, with Number Two sprawled across my lap. I am clutching at her neck with my fucked left hand, gripping as tight as possible, the gun in my right hand pressed against her right temple. And the safety catch is off.

"One more step, and her brains are all over the place!" I scream.

As any sound engineer Corvid have ever worked with will attest, I have a very loud voice; my microphone has to be set with a good twenty to twenty five percent less gain than normal. A writer on Mojo magazine once wrote that my voice *'...Switches effortlessly from a rich, gorgeously gothic baritone to a high pitched, nerve shredding squeal to a deeply disturbing, horrifically bassy death grunt...'*. So when I scream out my threat, the whole room is filled with my *'...high pitched, nerve shredding squeal...'*, so much so that Joseph stops, utterly shocked, and Numbers Three, Four and Five, run into him from behind. Joseph's gun falters, and I'm about to scream again, when law enforcement, summoned, I'm assuming, by the message I encoded into my filmed plea, plus the amount of noise I'm making now, make their presence felt.

The door to the farmyard smashes inwards, and helmeted, armoured Gardai burst in, shouting, "Armed Gardai! Drop your weapons!", while crashes and bangs and shouts from the next room suggest something similar is happening in there, presumably via the house's front door. Under the circumstances, I decide the best thing to do is to drop the gun, and put my hands on my head.

For a few minutes there is utter mayhem; uniformed, armed Gardai mill about putting cuffs on the kidnappers, pulling masks off and, when they find the Taipan and the automatic on the kitchen floor, shouting about guns. One young copper cuts the cable ties off my legs, freeing me from the chair, then uses bolt cutters to take the remaining handcuff off my right wrist. Then he helps me to my feet and guides me out into the farmyard, whispering, "Can I get your autograph later?

I'm a big fan!" as he does. He tells me as he ushers me across the farmyard that my message, mentioning the drone and Charles 'Chaz' Bolger's wallet, told the band immediately where I was, and the rest had been done with good old fashioned police methodology; stealth, infrared scanners, a battering ram and a lot of shouting. As we walk and he talks, I manage to snap my thumb back into place, suppressing a yelp of pain as I do.

I'm led to an ambulance where a young Lithuanian medic tends to my face, delighting in my fairly decent handling of her language. While we're chatting about the delights of Vilnius, a Garda Inspector arrives, and asks for some privacy.

"I've got to say, Mr Ogue," he says as the medic heads off into the house, "I'm pretty impressed. You basically sent us a message as to where you were. That's quick thinking."

"Well, I counted the turns when I was face down in the van with a bag over my head. So it was lucky I was right. But thanks to your guys too, probably just as well they acted when they did. I may well have shot one or more of them."

"Yes, one of my men tells me you were cable tied to the chair and still had handcuffs on one hand. So how did you manage to get that gun and put it against the young woman's head?

"I managed to slip one of the cuffs off and grab the gun. To be honest it all happened so –"

"Mr Ogue?" a voice cuts in. We look up to see another Garda, an older woman, in a uniform with somewhat more impressive decoration on its shoulders than the Inspector's. It's a face I recognise instantly, though I pretend not to.

"I'm Deputy Commissioner Susan Ryan," she says, "I need to ask you to come with me. There are some… sensitive issues to this case I need to discuss with you"

"Can it wait, Ma'am?" the Inspector says. "I still need to debrief Mr Ogue."

"I'm afraid it can't, Inspector. Don't worry, I'll get a statement from him. You concentrate on sorting the rest of the scene out."

I get the impression the Inspector isn't happy about this, but knows he's outranked.

"Ma'am," he says stiffly, then gets up and walks back towards the farmhouse.

"Oops," says Ryan. "I seem to have upset the Inspector. Never mind. Right, Mr Ogue, if you can come with me…"

I rise, and walk with her across the farmyard. As I do, I see Joseph and his minions being led out of the farmhouse, their masks off, their hands cuffed. They're just five ordinary people, late twenties, early thirties. The one I assume to be Joseph, his pale, round face angry, glares at me. I blow him a kiss.

Ryan guides me to a Gardai car. I'm installed in the passenger seat, Ryan gets behind the wheel, then after doing a three-point turn in the farmyard, we drive off along the lumpy, muddy track and onto the road.

"I'm impressed you got here so quickly, Susan" I say. "I take it you were the nearest VVO operative."

"Yeah, I got it off the Gardai intranet after your lot told Wexford CID when they got your video. I broke the land speed record getting down here from Dublin as soon as I heard about it."

"Cool, nice one. Have you got a phone I can use? I need to ring the band."

The guys are, of course, delighted I've been freed, and are already talking about writing songs about it. I promise to be there soon, and hang up.

"So, anything VVO need to be aware of? Anything that might make the kidnappers raise an eyebrow as to your age?" Susan asks.

"No. I did get smacked across the face with a gun, but I'll use a bit of makeup to keep the bruising going for a day or two longer in front of the band. And I don't think any of the kidnappers realised what I did with my thumb."

"What you did with your thumb?"

"Yeah, I dislocated it deliberately, meant I could get my hand out of the handcuff." I hold up my hand, and waggle the thumb. It's back to normal, if a little ache-y.

"Nice one! But listen," she says, "I promised that Inspector a statement. Can you reel off what happened? If we pull over somewhere, I'll record you on my phone.

You'll be a witness when it goes to trial, so we need to get your story straight."

"Actually, can we go back to the place where they grabbed me? I'd like to see if my bike is still there."

The bike is indeed still there, along with the helmet, and my smashed and useless phone. We load the lot into the back of Susan's car, then she sets the voice memo recorder going on her phone. I narrate the events of the last couple of hours, leaving out the bits about needling the kidnappers and dislocating my thumb. We run through it a couple of times, and she saves the one we reckon is the best.

"So, listen," Susan says as we pull out onto the road again, "I saw you on the telly this morning, that was interesting what you were saying about Cromwell and all that stuff about the land and the agriculture. Personal experience?"

"Kind of, yeah. I was here in the early 1600s, living the life of a rich Protestant in Dublin, then I went off to France for a bit, stayed there for a while, did the Sleep. Then I came back in the 1670s, and found that, as an alleged Protestant toff, I could buy great swathes of land dirt cheap from ex-soldiers from the New Model Army. They'd been given it in lieu of wages, and now they wanted to get out of Ireland because they kept getting attacked by Catholic guerrillas. So I bought most of Kilkenny and a good chunk of Wexford, then I had it legally transferred to a holding company in Dublin I set up, and then I got some of the original Catholic owners back on as tenant managers, gave them shares in the company in secret, and paid them dividends a couple of times a year. Bear in mind, the Catholics of Ireland were still getting a fucking terrible time from the English Prods, though they gave as good as they got too, there was some atrociously violent behaviour on both sides. I came and went a couple of times, came back as my son and grandson, yadda yadda yadda, you know how it is with us Immortals. I tried to use the land to help people in the 1840s, you know, during the Famine, and that worked a bit, and I got involved with the Tenant Right Leagues and I sold a lot of it off too. But I kind of had to leave in a hurry in 1852, I was attracting too much attention. By the time I got back, as a great nephew, the First World War was kicking off, so I bought what was left of the land from the holding company, just a hundred acres or so, and willed it to my alleged descendants. I've owned that last bit ever since."

"So where is it?"

"Not far now, in fact, take the next left, it's just a mile or so further."

Susan nods and smiles as we pull up at the big security gate at The Crow's Nest, and I lean out and tap the code in. The gate swings open, and we roll up the drive, stopping outside the front door. I tell her that the rest of the Corvid organisation thinks I was willed the land we built our base on by a great uncle, adding that we plan to donate it to the state to use as a musical school when we retire. I get out of the car, and pull the bike and helmet out of the back as three-fifths of Corvid plus Pete, Kev and Fat Freddie pour out of the front door.

"Thanks for the lift, Susan" I say, leaning back into the car. "Give's a shout in a few weeks, we'll go out for drinks and dinner. I'll tell you more about, well, this place." I indicate the locale with a wave of the hand. "It has some fascinating history behind it."

"I bet it does," she laughs. I close the door, and she drives away down the drive. Then I walk into the embrace of my musical family, and I burst into tears.

Jurgen Meyer in Berlin

I wondered which comedian had decided to call this year's European Very Very Old conference 'Lovers of German Opera Annual Convention 2016'. I presumed it was a nod to Some Like It Hot, that daft old film of 1959, where a group of Mafia bosses had booked a conference room in a hotel under the name 'Lovers of Italian Opera'. The comparison wasn't perfect of course; while VVO was very secretive, it wasn't a criminal organisation. Mostly.

The conference, held every four years, rotated between twelve different European venues, mostly historic, mostly owned by an Immortal. This time, it was being held at Charlottenburg Palace in Berlin. The most recent private owner, a scion of the Hohenzollern dynasty, had handed this vast palace over to the German people in the early twentieth century on the grounds that they could borrow back its East Wing every now and then; this was just such an occasion. Charlottenburg's original owner, Frederick the First of Prussia (1657-1713, allegedly) showed up for the conference most years, but this year I'd heard that he wouldn't be able to attend as he currently looked twenty-one and was on the brink of pop stardom in Brazil with his boy band HoHeZo.

At the appropriate door I had my RFID pass scanned by a Very Very Old guy. He put a tick on a printed list in front of him, then handed the pass back; I clipped it to my hoody. I assumed that, unlike me, he was a Senser, so no one who couldn't count their years in centuries would be allowed past. I also knew that the very latest anti-surveillance equipment would be installed throughout the building. Nodding thanks, I went on in to the ballroom.

"Joe! Joe Travis!" a voice exclaimed. I turned to see a tall, blonde woman standing there, arms spread wide, a huge grin on her face. She'd clearly Slept lately, because she looked no older than twenty-five.

"Janey Slater, good to see you," I said. "I didn't know you were with VVO now."

"Adriana Cellini these days," she tapped the pass clipped to her lapel. "And you're Jurgen Meyer now," she said, looking at mine. Then she hugged me tight and kissed my mouth wetly, a tiny hint of tongue on my upper lip. "I became a VVO agent two years ago, I'm based in Rome. My Italian is so good now that the Romans think I'm a local.

"Fantastic, I'm very impressed I said. "But look, I think we're about to start, I'm going to grab a coffee before we do. We can talk later."

"OK, but do make sure you're here at eleven on Sunday morning, I'm doing a presentation that will knock your socks off!" she exclaimed. Nodding assent, I extricated myself from her clutches and went over to the refreshment table.

There were upwards of 100 people in the room, each and every one an agent of the European part of Very Very Old, the organisation that deals with all matters Immortal; Paris was my usual stamping ground, though technically my section covered the whole of France. VVO has a website of course, www.veryveryold.com, much like Facebook, except with way better security, where Immortals – agents and non-agents – can chat and message each other, and indeed post clips of cats knocking vases off mantelpieces. It was through the site that details had gone out for the conference.

Not every Immortal is an agent of VVO, but every agent is an Immortal. It has a chairman, voted by agents every twenty years, and it was he who, as I sat down with my latte, stood up on stage, tapped on a microphone and said, "Good morning, fellow lovers of German opera," to scattered laughter. He continued, "I'm pretty sure I've met most of you, but just in case I haven't, my name is currently David Robinson, and I'm the head of Very Very Old in Europe. Welcome to the VVO conference 2016. We've got three days of business to get through, so without further ado, I'm going to introduce you to Mikhail Ostov, our conference coordinator, who will tell us what to expect."

Mikhail stood up and gave us an outline of the next three days. Today, Friday, was mostly matters financial and administrative, tomorrow was reserved for Science, Politics and Research and Development plus there was a party in the evening, and Sunday was... well, the last day of the VVO conference was always a bit of a free-for-all; anyone could stand up and talk about anything they liked. That was always the most interesting day, though the Saturday evening party was usually good fun too.

This morning though, I had something other than 'Last Wills and Testaments: the five best ways to leave everything to yourself when you "die"', 'Shell companies, the best and worst' and 'Your own personal bank?' on my mind, so as soon as the intro speech was over, and most people were heading off to one of the ten or so conference rooms in this wing, I slipped out, grabbed my leather jacket and crash helmet from the cloak room, and headed on into Berlin on my Honda that I'd ridden all the way from Paris, with an overnight stop the night before in Essen.

The traffic was light along Otto Suhr-Allee and through the Tiergarten so I was pulling up in the car park behind the Hotel Adlon just fifteen minutes later and lifting my kit from the panniers. I'd been tempted to take a roundabout route, going south of the Tiergarten and roaring along Kurfürstendamm, along the Landwehrkanal and up through Checkpoint Charlie, just for old time's sake, but I wanted to get the business in hand moving as fast as I could. I could go sightseeing next week, re-connect with a city I'd not been to in years; I had the suite in the Adlon booked for the next five nights.

In the suite's elegant sitting room, I sent a text message saying, 'An hour's time in the Adlon's first floor lounge?' and got one back inside a minute saying, 'OK C U there'. I shaved, cleaned my teeth, then swapped my jeans, shirt and hoody for something smarter. I stood in front of the full-length mirror in the bedroom: two metres tall, with narrow hips and broad shoulders, a long, rectangular face, short, jet black hair, very white skin, icy, grey eyes. I looked about forty.

I was slightly nervous about today's meeting. I hadn't seen Hannah Konrad since 1964 and we hadn't parted on good terms. She'd messaged me briefly a couple of weeks ago on Phnx, VVO's messenger app, so I'd replied, telling her I'd be in Berlin for the conference. As far as I could tell, she was a VVO user, not an agent. It also seemed she was still Hannah Konrad; I wondered if she'd Slept since we last saw each other. I certainly had, back in 1996.

At midday, I went downstairs to the first-floor lounge at the front of the hotel. I took a seat at a corner bay window overlooking Pariser Platz and the Brandenburger Tor, and ordered a double shot latte. The Platz was heaving with tourists, enjoying the sights on a warm end-of-summer morning.

I watched as two actors, one in an old style, German Democratic Republic National People's Army uniform with the insignia of an Oberst, the other dressed as a Soviet Praporshchik, stopped to pose for photos with a family of probable Americans who then gave them a handful of euros. I laughed to myself, wondering if the two guys, and indeed the Americans, knew that you would never, ever get a Colonel of the GDR walking together with a Russian Warrant Officer. I also noticed that the GDR uniform was missing its lapel flashes; I knew, because I'd seen the real thing in this city in the tense times before, during and after the Wall first went up. As my coffee arrived, I mused on those days, Ulbricht's stunning move taking the West by surprise, the face-off between American and Soviet tanks, and of course people's attempts, some successful, some not, to escape from East Germany.

I'd been there on the fifteenth of August 1961 when East German border guard Conrad Schuman made his famed run through the barbed wire and barriers from East to West. I didn't have my camera with me that day, but my friend Peter did, and it was he who took the iconic photo that came to grace hundreds of walls in West German houses, and maybe a few East German ones too.

This brought me back to Hannah Konrad and the last time we'd spoken. The very last thing she'd said to me was, "You're an ignorant capitalist lackey, paid in blood dollars by your American paymasters". The very last thing I'd said to her was, "Go and wallow in your idyllic workers' paradise then, you've got about fifteen years before the whole thing falls to the ground, and you either rejoin the West or we all get fucking nuked." Then I'd got out of bed, got dressed, and walked out of her flat in Neukölln.

And now, here she came. Standing at the top of the stairs, she hadn't spotted me yet, so for a moment I was able to study her. She clearly hadn't Slept since the last time I'd seen her; she looked a sprightly seventy. She was still beautiful; even at her alleged age she was turning the heads of those around her. Tall, slim, with long grey hair tied back in a ponytail, her sharp featured, almost feline face was kind and stern in equal measures. She was wearing a black cocktail frock with an open white man's dress shirt over it, and big Jackie O sunglasses pushed up into her hair. Then she spotted me, her bright blue eyes in evidence now. She threaded her way through the tables and chairs towards me. I stood.

"Hannah, hi. How are you?"

"Jurgen. Hello," she said. She put out a hand and I shook it, feeling slightly foolish. She put her bag on the table, and we sat.

"Can I order you a tea or a coffee?" I asked.

"Just a bottle of sparkling water please, to take away. Let's go into the Tiergarten." I waved a waiter over and gave him the order.

"Ok, sounds good to me," I said. There was an awkward silence, which I filled badly. "So what's happening, Hannah? Why the sudden desire to see me? I thought we split on pretty definitive political terms. No ambiguities in our last words, were there?"

She took a deep breath, then said, "No there weren't. But I need your help with something, something that's going to be pretty… difficult for both of us."

"Oh yeah? What's that?"

"I want to kill myself this evening, and I want you to help me do it."

"Wha — what? You… you want to die? After, what, two thousand years of life?"

"Yes, I do. Though before that I'd like to go for a walk with you, see a few sights, maybe come back here later for a massive fuck. But later on tonight, I'm going to drown myself in the Tegelersee."

"Jesus — uh, thank you," I broke off as the waiter delivered Hannah's water, and gave me a slip to sign. "You're serious about this, aren't you?"

"Yes."

"Why?"

"To be honest, Jurgen, there's a couple of reasons. But come on, it's a lovely day out, let's go into the Tiergarten."

So we walked out of the Adlon, across the Pariser Platz, and through the Brandenburger Tor. It was a lovely late September day, warm and sunny with a light breeze blowing, and once in the glowing green beauty of the Tiergarten we slowed to a snail's pace.

"So," she said, "Question. How old are you?"

"No idea of course. I don't remember being a child, I do remember bits and pieces from — what do they call it? Before Common Era, BC as used to be. I remember Gaius Trebonius, for instance, he stank. So I have to assume over two thousand years old."

"And how many people have you seen die?"

"Fuck, I don't know. Thousands."

"And how many have you killed?"

"I haven't counted. A hundred, maybe two hundred?"

"Who was the last person you killed?"

"I came across a guy raping a woman in a park in New York a few years ago. I was going to just grab him, give him a kicking, and hand him over to the police. But he came at me with a knife, so I took it from him and cut his throat. Called 911 and told them where they could find her then ran. But he was actually the first person I'd killed in, oh, decades. Not since a drunken Russian arsehole who tried to run me through with his bayonet here, near Tempelhof. 1952, I think."

Our first meeting, I with the British Army stationed in Wilmersdorf, she with the paramilitary Antifaschistische Aktion group operating out of Treptow, had been in 1955.

My squad had been on a joint patrol with the Americans in Kreuzberg when a riot had broken out just

189

inside the Soviet sector. We'd gone in to help the outnumbered Russian troops quell it, and my eye had been caught by one young civilian woman, dressed in Wehrmacht trousers, big Soviet boots and a black greatcoat. She'd just fought off two thugs, but was about to be attacked by three more, so I steamed in, kicked one so hard in the crotch he screamed like a girl, and caught the other a hefty punch to the forehead, ensuring loss of consciousness before he hit the ground; she'd pushed the third over and stomped on his face.

Then more of our guys and more Americans had arrived, so we threw as many people as we could get our hands on, including this intriguingly beautiful woman, into the back of several trucks, and drove them back to a big processing centre in Schönberg. The Soviets had complained bitterly that they needed to 'interview' everyone too, but we knew only too well the methods they used, and often did our best to keep prisoners out of their hands. While we were robust in our treatment of criminals, the Soviets were incredibly unpleasant; serious violence, rape and murder were routine in their notorious centres in Weisensee and Hohenschönhausen.

Hannah's papers had all been in order, and she wasn't on any wanted lists, so she'd been released after a few hours. I'd been in on her brief interrogation, and had been struck not just by her beauty, but her spirit, her intelligence, and her utter refusal to be kowtowed by us. And when I saw her walking towards the exit gate in the three-metre-high barbed wire topped chain link fence,

I'd walked up beside her and offered her a cigarette. A month later, three weeks after we'd started dating, two weeks after we'd started fucking, a Senser friend told me she was Very Very Old too. So I told her I knew what she was, and I told her what I was too.

And on and off over the next decade or more, we saw a lot of each other. Was it love? Yes and no, we were never actually 'in love', as far as I could tell. It certainly wasn't an exclusive relationship, we both saw other lovers. But although we were a world apart politically, we were comfortable in each other's arms. I was very sad when I heard that, a couple of months after we'd parted that last time, she'd finally gone back to East Germany.

And now here we were, sixty-one years later, she looking a fit seventy, me looking thirty years younger.

"And you don't get tired of it all?" she said. She took a swig from her water.

"The deaths? The killing? Yeah, sure. But it's all part and parcel of being Very Very Old. We have to deal with a lot more bad stuff than the mortals do, you know that. And we're good at it, we have to be, otherwise we'd lose our shit in a couple of hundred years and kill ourselves."

"Yeah, but some of us do. Remember Gary Smith? Gerhardt Hufschmied, as we knew him here?"

"Yep, I saw him, oh, ten years ago in Chicago."

"Drowned himself two years ago. Hired a rowing boat and stepped off it with two breezeblocks tied to his feet in the middle of the night. I was in the boat with him."

"What? You were... why? What the fuck?"

"I rowed the boat back to shore. And I want you to do the same for me."

"Fucking hell. I don't... I mean... drowning?"

"In deep water, with a heavy weight. Means that by the time the body is found it's rotted too much for some mortal pathologist to get much out of it about our, ah, unique physiology." That was a good point. Although we've researched ourselves to the limits of scientific analysis, we were automatically wary of a non-Immortal stumbling on our secret one day.

"Ah, hence the Tegelersee. Known for being pretty deep."

"Yep, twenty-two metres in the middle."

"But... look, why now, why not a hundred years ago, two hundred, a thousand? I mean, times have been much more brutal in the past. I saw Ivan the Terrible's reign close up, and that made modern day brutality look like a fucking rom-com. Ancient Egypt, Rome, the Aztecs, Genghis Khan. Why now?"

"Really? You need to be told?" She asked, sitting down on a bench.

I sat beside her. "Well, yeah. I mean it's a shit world, people are still killing the fuck out of each other, but then they always did."

"Surely you must have noticed the way this world is lurching inexorably to the Right? Racism is the new norm, Muslims are being demonised everywhere, anti-gay laws are being signed off all over the world, there are more and more Nazi organisations in every country in Europe, and plenty outside it too. Then there's a gangster in the Kremlin, and another one in Pyongyang, and they've both got nukes—"

"Well, yes, of course. But that's—"

"And it's only going to get worse. There's a damn good chance that disgusting piece of shit Donald Trump is going to become President of America and—"

"Oh, come on! Be serious. There is no way that awful old fucker gets to be C in C of the biggest nation in the West, no way at all. The Americans aren't that stupid."

"Don't you believe it, it's already happening in England. You know it's just three months since the stupids won the Brexit referendum in Britain and there's already a sharp spike in race related crimes?"

"I did but—"

"And no amount of dressing these fuckers up as the so-called Alt-Right can disguise the fact that they're just fucking Nazis. Remember, I was here, in Berlin, in the 1930s. I've seen this shit before. I guarantee, in the next year or two there'll be Nazis parading by torchlight somewhere in the Western World, and getting away with it. Meanwhile, we're busily poisoning the planet."

"Well, yes, but come on. Why die? Why kill yourself? That's a bit of an extreme reaction, isn't it? Why not fight against it? You were such an activist back when I knew you with Antifaschistische Aktion."

"And look how well that worked!" She drained her water, lobbed the bottle into a recycling bin and said, "Oh look, there goes another lump of single use plastic."

She stood, and stretched, and I stood too, and tried, and failed, not to look at her beautiful face and body, and think of what might happen in my hotel room later on.

"To be honest Joe – sorry, Jurgen, I'm just tired. Very very tired, very very tired and defeated and fucked off. The joy, the spark, has gone from my life. And there's a storm coming, and this time I don't want to be around for it. To be honest, I've been feeling like this for a couple of years now, but the last few months I've been coming round to Gary Smith's idea that I can stop it all by the simple expedient of being underwater with a couple of breezeblocks tied to my feet."

I had nothing to say to this, so I took her hand, and we stood for a few moments in silence. Finally, I sighed, and said, "So what do you want to do today?"

"Well, I've said goodbye to my mortal friends here. I've told them I'm off travelling round the world." An old favourite of ours when we head off for a Sleep. "I've turned all my properties into cash and given it to charities, mostly for the homeless, immigrants and abused women. My only possessions are the clothes I stand up in, and my car. I'm footloose and fancy free, so to speak. Let's make it up as we go along. If you've got any ideas, I'm all ears."

"You mentioned something about a massive fuck too. I like the sound of that."

She smiled, and said, "Easy, Tiger. End of the day. First, walking about."

So we walked north, and took a look at the Reichstag, Hannah telling me about that night in February 1933; she'd related it all before, but it didn't hurt to hear it again. She'd been at home, on nearby Invalidenstrasse, and had seen the glow.

"People were gathering all around it, watching the firefighters. Even then, I knew this was something dark, something bad. I never believed it was the Communists, even after Van der Lubbe confessed. I don't think anyone did. Anyway, the rest is history, the Enabling Act came along, democracy died, and soon the Nazis were untouchable. Then the War started, and soon my poor city was being bombed to bits. Your lot at night, the Americans by day—"

"Hardly my lot. I was only British by adoption at the time. And bear in mind, the Germans were bombing the living shit out of London and Coventry and Liverpool and—"

"Let's not get into who was bombing who, eh?" she said, taking my hand in hers again. "Let's get some ice cream."

We walked to Potsdamer Platz and bought cups of gelato from a street vendor.

"So you last Slept in 1950, yeah?" I asked.

"Yep. Disappeared for a few months, came back as my own great niece." Another standard move for us lot.

"Wow, that's what, sixty-six years. Long time to stay in one body, one timeline."

"Yep. But I love my city, I wanted to stay here, continuously, my life is very Berlin-centred. I've never had any actual family obviously, but Berlin, that's my family. Well, was. Until a couple of years ago, it was my intention to Sleep in, say, ten years' time, then maybe come back as my own great niece again. But tonight, I leave for good." And a shadow fell over us as we turned onto Leipziger Strasse.

We stood outside McDonalds on Friedrichstrasse by Checkpoint Charlie, watching tourists pose with more out of work actors playing border guards, this time American GIs – more historical inaccuracies. Even the checkpoint structure itself was fake; the original had been removed in 1990, and a replica placed there some years later, with added sandbags. Hannah then dropped her second bombshell of the day.

"You know I joined the Stasi in '67, don't you?"

"What?" I said, stunned. "What the fuck did you do that for?"

"I believed in Communism, you know that. That was why you and I fought more and more towards the end. And I wanted to protect it, and the GDR, from the West."

"Jesus, you really did swallow it, didn't you?"

"For a while, yes."

"And what did you do for them?"

"I was an officer in the so-called 'Main Administration for Struggle Against Suspicious Persons' section. Basically, I watched foreigners in East Berlin. Embassy staff, military personnel, tourists, you know, anyone who wasn't from the GDR. And that included Soviets, Hungarians, Czechs, anyone from the Eastern Bloc as well as the West. But especially Americans and Brits."

"So my name must have come up, I came into the East a couple of times, to our Embassy."

"In fact, you came into the East on six occasions, once in '68, three times in '69 and twice in 1970. After that you were rotated back to Britain, did a tour in Northern Ireland, left the army in 1972."

"For fuck's sake!"

"Yep. But you were small fry in Berlin, you just escorted people to the Brit embassy and back."

"Well yeah, mostly. I did a bit of smuggling too. Whiskey, cigarettes, luxury goods and so on, mostly for Party members. Plus, I escorted a VVO guy into East Berlin once, he was a very good Senser, and VVO thought we might be able to get more intelligence if we knew how many Immortals were working for you." The same guy who'd originally Sensed Hannah, we'd driven

197

him around East Berlin, especially near places we knew the Stasi used, but we'd quickly picked up a GDR Army tail, and when they started driving along beside us, eyeballing us, fiddling with their guns, we called it a day, and were back in the West within a couple of hours.

"And how many did you find? I mean, I only ever knew about three of us."

"He only picked up two that day. We did pick up two more a few years later."

"So we were watching you, you were watching us."

"Yep. How times change eh? Look out." We paused at the kerb as a parade of garishly painted Trabants trundled past, advertising something or other. Once they'd passed, we crossed, then walked on up Friedrichstrasse. At the junction with Unter Den Linden, we debated going to the Palace of Tears at Friedrichstrasse Bahnhof, but Hannah thought that would be too sad, so we turned right.

"Do you ever miss East Germany?" I asked.

"No! God no. Bear in mind, I left the GDR in 1974. I'd had enough. The infrastructure was sinking into entropy, the Stasi was the only growth industry in the country, we were in hock to the West up to our eyeballs, freedom basically didn't exist, so I left. Got myself a fake ID, went to Latvia and flew to Denmark, then to the States."

"Wow. So when did you come back?"

"I moved back permanently in 1990. This is my city. I've been here on and off since the late 1300s. I'm the same about this place as you are about Paris. I was never not going to come back once the GDR had collapsed and the Wall had been opened up again. Where were you on the eighth of November 1989?"

"Funnily enough, I was in Germany, in Bonn. I was at a computer trade fair, and the news came through about what was happening here, although it'd been on the cards all summer, what with Hungary and then Czechoslovakia. Where were you?"

"Washington. I was lecturing in German studies at the university, but I got caught out, I thought it'd be '90-'91 before it all fell apart. Then I saw the news coming in as it all kicked off. Got on a plane the day after the Wall came down."

As we approached Museum Island, we briefly toyed with the idea of popping into the Deutsches Historische Museum, maybe see if there were portraits of any Very Very Old friends, but we decided we were hungry, so at my suggestion, we crossed the island, and walked to Hackesche Höfe, one of Berlin's best known restaurants. We were shown to a table near the back, where we ordered schnitzel for me, salmon for Hannah, and beers. We clinked glasses and sipped our drinks.

"So have you got the logistics for, well, your last journey, sorted out?" I asked, setting my glass down.

"Yes. At about eleven p.m., we drive out to Reinickendorf in my car. There's a boat club with very poor security there, it shuts at ten p.m. I have heavy chain, a pair of handcuffs, a padlock and some bolt cutters in the boot of the car. We break into the club, steal a boat, and row out about three hundred metres. I put them on, kiss you goodbye, and I step overboard."

"You've got it all worked out then."

"Yeah, I drove over there during the week, scoped it out, there's a gap in the fence by the shore."

I couldn't think of anything to say, and was glad when, a minute later, our meals arrived.

The food was, of course, delicious, proper Berlineressen, and we took our time over it. By some sort of unspoken agreement, we didn't speak about what our day entailed, and how it was going to end, instead gossiping about various other Immortals we knew.

"No, she was caught giving some bishop a blowjob in the 1600s in Wales, so they tried to hang her." Hannah laughed. "She smiled and giggled as she hung there, so they cut her down. She got her hands free, kicked one of them in the throat, took his sword, ran another through, then she jumped on one of their horses and escaped. Hilarious!"

"Excellent. I always get a laugh out of her exploits. Any idea where she is these days?"

"Last I heard, she'd retreated to some tiny island in the Pacific. Maybe you should visit her there."

"Yep, I haven't seen her since, oh, the 1800s? Something like that."

"And what about you? Run into anyone interesting lately?"

"I met Jimmy Hoffa last year, he lives in London these days. Calls himself Antonio Morelli, works in a Michelin-starred Italian restaurant. Also ran into Big John Holmes last year in Portugal."

"The porn star? Cock down to his knees?"

"That's the one. I helped him fake his death when I lived in LA in the '80s. Nice guy, but he liked to live dangerously. We had quite an evening in Lisbon."

Our desserts arrived: a chocolate brownie for Hannah, a pear meringue for me.

"So where next?" I asked, tucking in.

"Could you bear the GDR Museum? It's just round the corner. Been meaning to take a look at it for years."

In the GDR Museum, Hannah said very little. I gave her some space, and let her wander off. I thought it was a pretty depressing place myself, full of cheap crap; it reminded me of the fixtures and fittings I'd seen on my forays into East Germany before, and indeed after the fall of the Wall.

"I suppose it's got to be the Fernsehturm next," Hannah said as we left the museum. She looked up at the iconic tower.

"Yep, cocktails at two hundred metres, sounds like a plan." We crossed the road, and walked along the Bundestrasse.

"You know," said Hannah as we headed into the Tower's entrance, "I need to correct something I said earlier."

"Oh yeah? What's that?" And for a moment, I hoped she'd changed her mind about suicide.

"You asked if I missed the GDR and I said no. That's not strictly true."

"It isn't?"

"No. I came to despise it, obviously, but being in the museum reminded me of a lot of the things I loved about the GDR. The sense of community, the sense of being part of something where everyone worked for the common good. For a short while in the '60s and early '70s it seemed like a good place to be."

"And yet you joined the Stasi."

"Yeah. I thought I could help protect the GDR from the demon West, the imperialist capitalist running dog lickspittles, blah blah blah."

"But the real demons were within, as far as I can tell."

"Yes and no. Ulbricht was OK for a long time, but towards the end he just started getting weirder and weirder. A lot of observers said he lost it the day Nikita Khrushchev died, and the GDR lost it with him. And a lot said that when Honecker took over he was handed a poisoned chalice, and his utter ineptitude just accelerated the decline and fall. And we can forget about Krenz, he was almost a… what d'you call it? A patsy, installed to take the fall when the Wall came down."

We bought our tickets from a machine in the lobby, and joined the queue for the lifts. We stayed quiet in the crowded lift, and when we got to the bar, were lucky enough to grab a table for two right at the windows, just as a pair of elderly men vacated it. I ordered a Dirty Gibson; Hannah asked for a Brandy Alexander.

"And of course, the other thing I miss," Hannah said, "is the tradecraft."

"The tradecraft? What d'you mean?"

"The tricks and stuff we used in the Stasi. You know, the gadgets and code words, the dead letter drops, I mean, it wasn't exactly James Bond, but it was almost fun."

"I thought you said you just watched people," I said, watching the barman building our drinks.

"Well yes, but sometimes, if we couldn't prove someone was a spy, we pulled some sort of trick to keep them out, you know, just in case. The old purloined radio trick, for instance." She paused as our drinks were set down in front of us. We clinked glasses, sipped appreciatively, and she went on. "We'd stop the guy in the street, frisk him, check his papers, secrete a crappy little transistor radio in his bag, then send him on his way. Then when he got searched going back over the border, he'd be accused of shoplifting the radio. We'd fling him in a van, take him back to HQ, give him the third degree about being a shoplifter and a spy and hoodlum and a... oh, you know all the rest. Then we'd graciously release him without charge, ban him from the GDR for life, and throw him back to the West."

"Yeah, we had a few that happened to. Almost all of them weren't spies though."

"Almost?" she laughed.

"Almost. In fact, with the non-spies it became a badge of honour."

"Something to dine out on?"

"Absolutely. 'I'm such a danger to Communism, they've banned me from the East…' though they never added '… with a shitty little trick even the most amateur of agents would pick up on the moment it happens'. My last visit, it was tried on me, but I just checked my bag, found the radio and threw it in the river. Border guard went through my bag with a fine-tooth comb, but never found it. Pissed him off mightily."

We laughed together, then fell silent for a moment.

"This is weird," I said eventually.

"How d'you mean?"

"Well, here we are, having a leisurely drink, looking out at this stunning view. Yet it's going to end with you dying."

"Yep. What better way to spend my last day?"

"Look, I'm going to ask you this twice, once now, once later. Is there anything I can say or do to make you change your mind?"

"No, Jurgen, there isn't. I am quite settled with the idea."

"OK. But I will be asking you one more time."

"OK. Thank you."

More gossip, more small talk, more chit chat. I couldn't work out whether I felt happy or sad, angry or calm, in love with Hannah or... well, anything. It was a surreal position to be in – sitting drinking excellent cocktails two hundred metres above ground level with a two thousand-year-old woman who wanted to die a few hours later, gossiping about a sixteenth century British king who these days ran the best surf shop in Hawaii.

Until today I'd never heard of an Immortal killing themselves. Killed by mortals, yes, a few times, accidental deaths too. I lost an Immortal lover in Renaissance Rome when she was crushed to death by a collapsing church wall. But suicide? I'd never heard of an Immortal doing such a thing.

It made my skin crawl. A few years before, I'd watched a British science fiction TV show where an Immortal man suddenly became mortal, and it made me sick with anxiety, while a 1980s film, set in this very city, where an angel voluntarily gave up his immortal status after falling in love with a mortal woman made me cry, and not in a good way. I wasn't a good sleeper at the best of times, that's sleep, not Sleep, but for the next week or two I barely slept a wink. I was, it had to be admitted, terrified of death, and I suspected many other Immortals were too.

Meanwhile, Hannah was rattling her empty glass and saying "Ahem. Your turn to order"

An hour later, we were strolling, arm in arm, along Unter den Linden, in a pleasant alcoholic haze. I'd had a sudden craving for cigarettes, so I'd bought some, lit two, and handed one to Hannah. She'd been a heavy smoker back in the fifties, but these days barely indulged at all.

"So where next?" I asked. She looked at her watch.

"Back to The Adlon, I think. Another cocktail, then up to your room for some excellent sex."

We never did have that cocktail. By the time we entered the hotel, we were talking dirty about what we wanted to do to each other. We kissed with tongues in the lift, our groins grinding together, and we were barely through the door to my suite before we were tearing each other's clothes off.

I woke from a sleep so deep I almost expected to be twenty years old again. I sat up. It was dark. The glowing face of the bedside display told me it was twenty past ten.

"Hey, Schlafmütze," Hannah's voice came from the sofa by the window. I got up and went over to her; she was naked, looking ethereally beautiful in the light coming in through the balcony windows. She'd opened the door, so a slight breeze blew in. She patted the sofa.

"Hey," I said, sitting beside her. "How's it going?"

"Oh, OK. Just, you know, last thoughts." She snuggled into my side, her hand in my lap. I put an arm around her while she took hold of my cock. "We're going to have to get going soon, my car is a few streets away. You OK to drive?"

"Yeah, sure. No probs."

"You can keep the car if you like, or give it away."

"Cool."

We sat in silence for a few minutes, then, seeing what her hand was doing to me she asked, "One last fuck?"

Half an hour later, we were in her Beemer heading through the Tiergarten. She was looking out the right-hand window, I was driving. I felt awful; I'd come very close to just refusing to drive her anywhere, but knowing that she'd just call a cab, I decided to go to Reinickendorf with her. At least this way the last thing she saw before the waters closed over her would be a friendly face.

We got there a little before eleven thirty. I parked the car on a quiet stretch of the wooded coast road, and we got out. She opened the boot, and took out a large, obviously heavy, sports bag. Then she gave me the car keys, saying "This way," and walked off into the trees.

We climbed through a gap in the chain link fence, and walked quietly onto the pier at the darkened boating club. She hauled the bolt cutters out of the bag and cut the chain that secured the boats together and climbed into the last one and sitting on the stern seat. And I followed her, then took up the oars, and rowed us under the bridge and out into the moonless night.

We barely spoke. Guided by her, I rowed, she looked out over the mirror-calm waters, and every now and then checked her phone's GPS. And then she said, "Here, more or less," and I back-watered with the oars, and brought us to a standstill. She dropped her phone overboard, then opened the bag at her feet, and started to haul the chains out. I didn't help as she started to wrap it around her ankles. She padlocked it, making sure it was tight, leaving a foot or so of chain which she attached to a set of handcuffs she then snapped shut on her wrists. She hauled herself up onto the transom of our little craft.

"One thing," she said. "Please don't tell any of our people about this. I don't want to… well. Just don't, please."

"Yeah. Yeah, no problem." It was a decision I'd already made.

"OK, I'm ready to go," she said.

"Which means I ask you one last time; is there anything I can say or do to make you change your mind?"

"No," she said. "But you can kiss me goodbye."

I leaned forward, and we kissed, very gently. Then she pulled back, said, "Goodbye, my love," and before I knew it, she'd tipped herself over backwards and, with a surprisingly small splash, she was gone.

"Auf wiedersehen, meine Liebe," I whispered.

I stayed there for another hour or so, smoking cigarettes, fiddling with my phone and, for a few minutes, crying. Hannah didn't reappear.

I didn't go back to Charlottenburg Palace till Sunday. After driving back to The Adlon and leaving Hannah's car in the car park, keys in the ignition, I holed up in my suite and spent what remained of Friday, and most of Saturday getting trashed. With a couple of grams of coke from a bellhop and a couple of minibars' worth of vodka, gin, whiskey and brandy, I chain-smoked cigarettes, cried, and generally was more miserable than I think I've ever been. I tried to get my act together on Saturday evening, and went downstairs to one of the hotel restaurants for dinner but when tears started to form in my eyes as I perused the menu, I knew it was useless. I got up, went back to my room, and dined from another bottle.

On the Sunday morning, I washed and shaved, dressed in a clean pair of jeans and a clean white shirt, and, after a light breakfast in the hotel's dining room, I climbed onto the Honda, and headed to the Palace.

I slipped into the ballroom at a few minutes to eleven and took a seat at the back. Adriana Cellini was already on the stage. I sat and sipped my coffee and tried not to think about Hannah Konrad.

At precisely eleven o'clock, Adriana said into the microphone, "Hello, my name is Adriana Cellini, I'm with the Rome office of VVO, and I have rather an amazing announcement. First, a bit of back story. I met my current partner, Celine, a little over four years ago. She's Very Very Old too, she Sensed me in a bar in Milan. We've been together ever since; we are going to get married fairly soon.

Back at the end of March, we met this rather lovely young mortal man, Tom from Idaho, in the Villa Borghese, and, well, we seduced him, took him back to our place, and had an excellent evening's sex." There were cheers, laughter and wolf whistles, Adriana smiled and held out her hands to quieten us down. "We sent him on his way next day, and that was that. Or was it? Hang on, I'm just going to call Celine, she's stayed away from the Conference for the last couple of days, but she's waiting outside now." She took her phone out, tapped it, waited a couple of seconds, then said, "You can come in now."

The doors behind me opened, and I turned to see a young-looking, blond woman coming in. She was dressed in a big, dark blue kaftan and sandals. She walked up the aisle to the stage, stepped up onto it and went to stand beside Adriana. She leaned towards the mic, looking self-conscious.

"Hello, my name is Celine Rodean," she said. Then she turned to Adriana and said, "It's probably best if I showed, rather than told, wouldn't you say?" Adriana, smiling, nodded. And Celine stepped to the very front of the stage, undid a couple of buttons on her kaftan, and pulled it off over her head, dropping it on the floor. And all around the ballroom came gasps and exclamations, the sounds of shock and surprise and chairs falling over; I found myself standing, my jaw hanging open, staring at her, as she stood there in sandals, knickers and bra.

Because she was quite clearly pregnant.